Razor's Edge

Nikki Tate

orca sports

ORCA BOOK PUBLISHERS

Library and Archives Canada Cataloguing in Publication

Tate, Nikki, 1962-
Razor's edge / written by Nikki Tate.

(Orca sports)
ISBN 978-1-55469-167-8

1. Horses—Juvenile fiction. I. Title. II. Series: Orca sports

PS8589.A8735R39 2009   jC813'.54   C2009-903045-4

Summary: Travis and his friends train and race horses at a harness-racing
track. When someone starts hacking off the horses' tails, Travis must solve
the mystery before he loses everything he has worked for.

First published in the United States, 2009
Library of Congress Control Number: 2009928874

Orca Book Publishers gratefully acknowledges the support for its publishing
programs provided by the following agencies: the Government of Canada
through the Book Publishing Industry Development Program and the
Canada Council for the Arts, and the Province of British Columbia through
the BC Arts Council and the Book Publishing Tax Credit.

Cover design by Teresa Bubela
Cover photography by Getty Images
Author photo by E. Colin Williams

Orca Book Publishers
PO Box 5626, Stn. B
Victoria, BC Canada
V8R 6S4

Orca Book Publishers
PO Box 468
Custer, WA USA
98240-0468

www.orcabook.com
Printed and bound in Canada.
Printed on 100% PCW recycled paper.

12 11 10 09 • 4 3 2 1

For Bill and Marian Young

chapter one

"What the—?"

I step into the stall and run my hand along Romeo's back and over his rump. The handsome gray gelding looks back over his shoulder. I reach for his tail. Or rather, the place where his magnificent cream-colored tail used to be. Someone has cut the whole thing off.

"Ryan! Get in here!"

My buddy Ryan's hulking form fills the stall doorway. "Travis, why are you yelling?

We can't afford another vet—" He stops mid-sentence and steps into the stall beside me. "What the—?"

"That's what I said! Who would do something like this?"

Ryan turns slowly, studying the mess of wood shavings, manure and bits of dropped hay.

"I already looked," I say. "There's not a single hair left."

Ryan shakes his big head from side to side. "It doesn't make any sense. Why would someone steal a horse's tail?"

"Hell if I know."

Stupidly, we both look around the stall again.

"It's gone, man. Like really gone." Ryan jerks his head toward the open stall door. "What about the others?"

"I just got here. I came in to get Romeo's feed tub and—" We both stare at the horse's scraggly stump of a tail.

Ryan moves toward the door. I'm right behind him. I grab a manure rake from where it leans against the wall in the barn aisle.

"Hey, Finnegan," Ryan says, unlatching the next stall door in the long row. "Show me your backside, buddy."

Still clutching the rake handle, I follow Ryan inside.

"I guess whoever did it doesn't like black tails," he says.

Finnegan swings his rear in my direction. His black tail swooshes behind him. It's long and full, reaching well past his hocks.

"What about Dusty Rose?"

Ryan is about to push past me again when he spots the manure rake in my hands. I'm holding it in front of me, trying to look dangerous.

"What are you doing? The mucking can wait..."

"Uh..."

Ryan's eyebrows push together. Then he laughs. "Good to know you've got my back!"

We check on our other two horses. Dusty Rose and Dig in to Win are both fine.

"What was so special about Romeo's tail?" I say when we're back out in the aisle.

Ryan shrugs. "He's the only gray horse in this barn. And his tail was long and thick."

True enough. When Romeo is flying along at full speed, he carries his tail high enough that it whips around my hands when I'm driving. We had actually talked about wrapping it so it didn't get caught up in the sulky during a race. The lightweight racing carts the horses pull are dangerous enough without extra interference from an out-of-control tail.

"Does Jasper know yet?" I ask.

"Not yet. He's probably at The Bog."

"I'll go find him," I offer. "I need another coffee. Do you want anything?"

Ryan shakes his head. "I'll get started here."

Sure enough, Jasper's at The Bog, the coffee place the horsemen use at Blackdown

4

Park Racetrack. It's not nearly as fancy as the restaurants and casino over in the grandstand. The coffee tastes like swamp water, but the café is handy and at this hour of the morning, anything hot and caffeinated goes down well.

The youngest partner in our harness-racing business is impossible to miss. He's six foot five and stick skinny. As usual, Jasper's wearing a saggy black T-shirt. Before he even turns around I know the kind of thing that will be on the front. Jasper's tastes run toward skulls, spiders and blood-dipped daggers.

When the three of us stand together, it's like someone took the average of the other two to get me. I'm not as tall as Jasper or as big around as Ryan. My hair is lighter than Jasper's thick dark mop and not as wild as Ryan's blond curls.

The reserve where Jasper lives is right next to the track, so you'd think he'd get to the track first every morning. Wrong.

"Hey, Jasper!"

"Hey, Travis." When Jasper turns away from the counter, I am eye-to-eye with three bubble-headed aliens staring back at me from his chest. As usual, he looks like he crawled out from under a rock.

"You're not going to believe what happened to Romeo."

"What's wrong?"

"He's fine. Well, fine in a bald kind of way."

"What are you talking about?"

"Someone stole his tail."

Jasper laughs, a huge loud laugh that shakes his whole body. "Yeah, right."

"No, I'm serious. Someone cut it off."

"Romeo's tail?" Jasper can't stop laughing. "Good one! April Fools' Day to you too!"

"April Fools' Day?" He's right. Today is April first. "Jasper, this is no joke. His tail is totally gone!" I doubt he'll believe me until he sees for himself.

Jasper fights hard to pull himself together. "That's crazy!"

"Yeah, it is crazy. But that's what happened." I tell Jasper the whole story, and by the time I'm done he isn't laughing anymore.

"What kind of sicko would chop off a horse's tail?" he asks.

All I can do is shrug.

chapter two

"We need to win a race so you can buy new boots," Ryan says, poking the butt end of a driving whip into a hole in the heel of my rubber boot.

"We need to win a race so we don't have to sell a horse," Jasper says. He runs his finger down the page in his notebook.

Jasper may be the baby in our group, but he's the one who's actually organized enough to keep track of what we're spending and how much we're bringing in.

That makes it sound like our harness-racing business actually makes money. Most months we're lucky to cover our bills. Even so, we try to run our racing stable right. The business plan—and we do have one—is to start making a profit by the end of this year. To do that we need to keep our costs down, look after our horses ourselves and finish in the top five in any races we enter. The purse money is always split among the top five horses. Of course, winning pays the most, but even with decent horses it isn't as easy as it sounds.

So far, other horse owners haven't been too impressed with our efforts. We don't have any horses owned by clients, unless you count Finnegan. Ryan's uncle bought him for us when we were getting started a year ago and, technically, he still owns him. We haven't earned enough yet to pay him back.

We don't mind all the work we have to do, but none of us is crazy about meetings. We'd rather be doing stuff with the horses.

But Jasper insists that we meet every Monday to figure out who's doing what during the coming week. Our tack room in A-barn is really too small for our meetings, but we have them here anyway.

Recently, the meetings have been pretty depressing.

Ryan tips his chair back and leans his head against the wall. He closes his eyes and sighs. The chair creaks a little under his weight.

"I'm getting paid Friday," he says. Ryan has a part-time job at the gas station.

Jasper looks at me and raises an eyebrow.

"Not until next week," I say. "And it won't be much, because I put last week's feed on my tab."

I work Thursday evenings at the Chick-a-Biddy Tack and Feed Emporium. The good news is that I get a discount on horse feed. The bad news is—well, there's lots of bad news. First, they don't pay well. Second, the tack part of the store doesn't carry much that's useful to us. Because we're harness racers, we don't ride our horses, we drive them. Which brings me to the third thing about my job that makes me crazy: the people who come in and spend tons of money are all these middle-aged women who love dressage and treat their horses like kittens. They wear top hats and coattails at horse shows where they ride their fancy horses in perfect circles. Where's the thrill in that? I can understand how the show jumpers or eventers get excited about what they do. Leaping over big fences is almost as dangerous as driving a horse in a harness race. Not that any of us want to see anyone—horse or human—get hurt. But seriously, how hard can it be to sit there and look pretty?

The only good thing about those dressage women is that some of them have daughters my age who are kind of cute. Sometimes they come in wearing their tight riding pants and high boots. That part of my job is great, especially when the girls bend over to go through the bargain tubs at the back of the store.

"Travis?"

"What?"

"I asked how much you can put in next week."

"Maybe enough to get Dusty's feet trimmed and those shoes re-set."

Jasper nods and makes a note. "I'll call and make an appointment with Dan."

Dan is our farrier, the guy who keeps our horses' feet in good shape. He's also one of Jasper's eight hundred cousins. Okay, he doesn't really have eight hundred cousins, it just seems that way. However many cousins he has, at least half of them work at the track. Some of the older guys don't like to hire guys from the reserve. I don't get that. Dan is a good farrier. He's patient with the horses and never complains when we call him to replace a thrown shoe or if he has to wait to get paid.

My dad says that you can tell a lot about a man by how he deals with a horse. It drives my mom crazy when he says stuff like that. "What about women?" she wants to know.

Jasper finishes punching numbers into his calculator, writes something in his notebook and flicks his pen across the card table. "You might not have to chip in anything if we can get a couple of decent finishes on the weekend," he says to me.

Ryan laughs and his chair *thunks* forward. "We can hope!"

"That would be a good name for a horse," Jasper says.

"That's what we should have called our stable...," I mutter.

"Get over it, would you?" Ryan pokes me with the whip. "If we can't feed our horses, we won't need any kind of name for our stable."

Ryan, Jasper and I call our business Three Musketeers Racing Stable. It's not

13

the most original name, but we were desperate. It doesn't seem like it would be that hard to come up with a name, but man, we were ready to kill each other. Jasper wanted something like the Fanged Avengers Racing Team. That might have been okay except that when you see the initials by themselves—FART—the name wasn't going to strike fear into the hearts of other trainers. Then Ryan said we should combine our names somehow. Ryvisper, Jatran and Trysper were some of the names we came up with. Since we couldn't remember how to spell them from one day to the next we didn't think any of those would work either.

My dad inherited both his own name and the name his horses race under—Geoff Russell Racing—from my grandfather, Geoff Russell Sr. Dad's been in the business forever, but the best suggestion he came up with for us was Fat Chance Racing Stables. Jasper said my dad was just worried we were going to amaze everyone with our stunning horses. That hasn't exactly happened.

When Jasper finally suggested Three Musketeers, Ryan and I looked at each other and said, "Yeah, fine." It's not like we were crazy about the name, but we weren't going to live long enough to agree on another one.

"So, who's jogging what horse?" I ask Jasper. It's great that I don't have to worry about the schedule. As long as I am more or less awake when I show up, I do what I'm told. Jasper is so well organized he always has a plan.

"I'll do Dusty Rose, you do Finnegan," Jasper says to me and scribbles our names down in the book. "Ryan's on stalls."

I glance at my watch. It's getting late—nearly 6:30 AM. If we don't hurry up I'm going to be late for school. Mondays suck, pure and simple. Only three months to go and grade eleven will be done. Ryan is pretty happy he graduates this year. I'd feel sorry for Jasper, who is only in grade ten,

15

but he actually seems to like going to school. Freak.

I stand up and stretch. Mondays suck, but if we want Three Musketeers to survive, we need to win races. To win races, we need fit horses.

"Easy there, Travis—your spuds don't have legs." My dad nods at the heap of food on my plate. Roast potatoes. Roast carrots. Roast pork. And roast Brussels sprouts. Mom knows our favorites and regularly bribes us with food. She wants us to find some time to work on the new deck. I try to slow down, but it's hard not to shovel in the food when it's so good.

"What about this weekend?" Mom asks.

Dad and I keep our heads low over our plates. "This is delicious, Bev," Dad says. I grunt in agreement.

"Flattery will get you two nowhere. I need your help—I can't build the deck by myself. I thought you said you could take next Monday off, Geoff."

Next Monday is one of those teacher development days, so I don't have school. It's also the day after the first of the Delgatto Stakes races. Dad has a filly running. I bet that's what he's thinking about.

What I'm thinking about is how much Jasper, Ryan and I can make between now and the fifteenth. That's when we have a payment due on Dig in to Win. We couldn't afford to pay his full price when we bought him last month. Tino Owen gave us a deal and said we could make a couple of payments. Tino might seem generous, but he has the biggest biceps I've ever seen. Last year he threw a hammer through his tack-room window when his groom didn't show up for work. I wouldn't put it past him to use that hammer to smash kneecaps if we don't pay on time.

"Boys?" Mom reaches over and touches my dad's arm. "Geoff, you promised."

Dad lets out his breath slowly. "Yeah, I know." He turns to me. "Travis, you in?"

"Fine. What about Angela?"

"Me?" My little sister is the queen of pink. She likes to pretend she can't swing a hammer, shovel out a stall or handle a paintbrush.

"Yeah, you. You'll be the first in line when we have a barbecue on the new deck."

"I'd love to help, but we have that three-day meet over in Hickston."

Angela is a gymnast. She is stronger than some of the guys in my class. Her eight-pack is scary. She's thirteen and does insane things on the balance beam.

"We can manage without Angela if you two are going to be here," Mom says, looking from me to Dad. "Leave me your truck some afternoon between now and then. I'll pick up another load of lumber."

Dad nods, his mouth full of roast something. Mom is one of those skinny little women smart people don't mess with.

"Good. Thanks, boys. Do they know anything more about the tail thief?" Mom asks, switching gears. Dad is already on to the next mouthful. He's one to talk about eating too fast.

I shake my head. "I was at the office, and Jack Krueger said he was going to file a police report."

"How many did they steal?" Angela asks.

"Three." I hold up fingers as I count. "Romeo. Jill's little filly—the one that was off in the fall with the hock problem. And Rocket's good horse—Big Man in Town."

"That is so creepy," Angela says. "What kind of weirdo would chop off horse tails? Maybe they're, like, in a cult or something. Maybe they eat babies."

"Angela, please!" Mom turns back to me. "Do they have any ideas?"

Dad shrugs. "They all had good tails."

"Good tails?" Angela laughs. "As opposed to what?"

"As opposed to scrawny tails. They were all long and thick."

Angela looks unconvinced.

"And all white...," I offer.

Most Standardbreds are bays, various shades of brown with black manes and tails. It *is* strange that someone would carefully select the three gray horses at Blackdown Park, the only ones with light tails.

Mom helps herself to more salad. She picks out the mushrooms and transfers them to Dad's plate. "What are the guys in the office going to do about it?"

Dad shrugs again and slices off a healthy piece of pork. "What can they do about it? I guess report it to the cops."

"What about extra security?"

"Honey, extra security costs money. You know the track keeps crying poverty. Krueger says they're thinking about cutting back to two race days a week."

I eat faster. Just the thought of less racing makes me worry more. And when I worry, I eat.

"Was that apple pie I saw on the counter?" I ask.

Mom nods, pushing her empty plate away. "Life's short. Enjoy dessert."

"With ice cream," we chorus.

chapter three

"I swear he's faster without a tail," Jasper says, guiding Romeo back into the barn the next day. Jasper has just given the horse a fast workout.

For the thousandth time, I wish that Jasper were old enough to get his license to drive in races. He's got this feel for the horses that's kind of unreal. Somehow he knows exactly how hard to push, exactly when to push, and exactly when to just sit tight and wait. And he never loses his cool.

It's like there's the soul of an ancient driver trapped in Jasper's sixteen-year-old body.

"First quarter in twenty-six." When Jasper does that, it blows my mind. Most people need to check a clock to figure out how fast the horse is covering each quarter mile. Not Jasper. It's like he has a stopwatch in his brain. If he says Romeo covered the first quarter mile in twenty-six seconds, you know he's right.

I unsnap the quick hitch as Jasper moves around Romeo's other side, gathering the long driving lines and moving toward the horse's head.

"We just need him to race like that on Sunday." Jasper gives Romeo's head a rub and moves him a step forward as I lift the shafts high and push the training cart out of the way.

"Great job, Jaspie!" Ryan says, slapping Jasper on the back. "Dusty's ready to go."

The filly stands in her crossties, her harness on. I maneuver the cart behind her and snap her in as Jasper reaches her head and slips off the halter we've put on over her driving bridle.

Meanwhile, Ryan has stripped the harness off a steaming Romeo. He leads the gelding forward down the barn aisle, starting the process of cooling out the sweating horse. Romeo's sides puff in and out, and he snakes his head down and forward as they set off.

Driving from the ground beside the cart, Jasper makes smoochy noises to Dusty. She steps forward, and Jasper walks along behind the cart, holding the long driving lines. When they clear the big double doors halfway down the barn and get outside, Jasper hops onto the seat without missing a beat. Casually he braces one foot against the front of the jog cart. The other leg dangles down, his boot sole not quite touching the ground.

He looks completely relaxed, but I know he is already reading the filly's body language, testing to see how responsive she is to the signals he telegraphs down the lines.

Dusty is our least consistent horse. Some days she's amazing—runs her heart out. Other days, it's like she doesn't even know she's a racehorse. Just like human athletes, what a horse is thinking and feeling affects how it performs. Jasper is already a master at figuring that out.

While Jasper takes Dusty Rose out for her training session and Ryan strolls around the barns with Romeo to cool the horse down, I grab a manure rake. Dusty will be gone for about twenty minutes—exactly enough time for me to muck out her stall, dump the wheelbarrow full of manure and make a trip to the shavings pile for a barrow full of fresh bedding. While I'm doing the bedding, I let water trickle into her bucket. The last job is to fill her hay net. If I time it right, I'll have just hooked her net back up when Jasper gets back.

We take turns doing the different jobs. We all have our trainer's licenses so we can drive the horses during work-outs. Sometimes it feels like we were born attached to manure rakes and wheel-barrows. That's what happens when you're practically raised at the track.

Pippa Rochester sticks her head into the stall just as I'm about to pick up the first pile of manure.

"Hey, Travis. Got any work for me?"

Pippa is not quite twelve, but she's been working around the barn for as long as I can remember. Her dad is Rocket Rochester, a guy who has been driving Standardbreds forever. "I wish!"

"When are you guys gonna win some more races?" she asks. "I need more work! The sale is next month!"

"Sorry, Pippa. Not today. Check again on the weekend. Maybe you could paddock for us?"

The minute the words are out of my mouth I want to suck them back. Lots of the younger teenagers help in the paddock, the long barn where the horses are taken before they race. That's where they are hitched to the race bikes—sulkies that are lighter and faster than the jog carts we use for training. You have to be in the paddock early, before you're allowed to head out to the track. Dusty and Dig in to Win both race on Saturday, which makes it tough to be in more than one place at once.

The problem is, kids under twelve aren't allowed in the paddock. The rules don't care that someone like Pippa knows more about harness racing than most people ever will.

I dig around in my jeans pocket and pull out a handful of coins. "This is all I have..."

"All you have? Or all you want to give me?"

"Both. Take it or leave it."

Pippa leans over and pokes at the coins in my palm. Apparently, there are enough there to make her happy.

"Fine. But don't expect me to muck stalls for this every day."

I hand her the manure rake and step out into the aisle.

"Nice one, Russell."

Sassafras Calloway leans against the last stall, idly stroking Finnegan. The gelding has his big head practically in her lap.

"Hi, Sassy."

"That's probably breaking every child labor law in the books, you know." She nods toward Dusty's stall. Pippa is so short that when she bends over to scoop a forkful of manure she disappears completely. "And that's Sassafras to you."

There's no point in arguing. Every other week Sassy changes her mind. Not just about her name. Every week she does something crazy with her hair. This week it's jet black. She's put something in it to make all these pointy tips in her bangs. The points line up across her forehead. Even with her strange hair and her baggy sweaters, Sassy always looks cool. All the guys, including me, think Sassy is hot.

"Is that a picket fence on your head?"

"Ha ha." She snaps her gum, and Finnegan's ear twitches. "I need a favor."

"What kind of favor?"

28

"My cat's sick."

"Good one. What—did he eat your homework?"

Sassy tips her head to the side and narrows her eyes. "Jerk. No, she's sick. She got into my purse and ate a bunch of chocolate."

"Chocolate?"

"Really expensive chocolate."

"Chocolate's harmless."

"Just shows what you know. It's not harmless to cats. Especially small cats. Especially dark chocolate. Argentina's at the vet. I have to go and pick her up. Can you help me out or not?"

"Your cat is seriously at the vet because it ate some chocolate?"

Sassy draws in a deep breath and opens her mouth as if she's going to let me have it with one of her famous blasts of creatively foul language. Instead, her lower lip begins to wobble and her eyes fill with tears.

"Never mind. I'll ask someone else."

She spins around and stalks off.

"Sassy! I thought you were kidding! I've never heard of that before. I eat chocolate all the time!"

"You are not a cat!" Sassy says, still walking.

I jog after her. "Hey—" I reach out and touch her arm, and she waves me away. Her other hand reaches up and wipes her cheek.

"Sassy—I'm sorry. What do you need me to do?"

"I don't know who else to ask. I need a ride to the vet." She bites her bottom lip and keeps walking. "My mom's car broke down again."

I grab her arm and this time she doesn't jerk away. "Wait here. I'll get Pippa to tell the guys where I went."

She doesn't say anything, but she waits for me. I'm back a couple of minutes later. "Let's go."

"It was so disgusting," she says when we're in my truck. "Argentina was acting all weird—shaking and trembling—and then my mom saw the chewed wrapper and my purse was on the floor and we figured out what happened." The words come out in a rush and then she starts to cry again. "I thought she was going to die."

I keep my eyes on the road and reach past Sassy's knee to fish out some McDonald's napkins stashed in the glove box. "Here."

"Thanks."

"Mom called the vet and they told us to give her hydrogen peroxide and milk to you know, make her puke...but she couldn't really puke. I don't think we got it all down her throat. And my mom is, like, freaking out and I'm trying to carry the cat out to the car and my mom doesn't want Argentina puking in the car and I'm screaming at her to never mind the towels and just get her keys and let's go..." Sassy closes her eyes and leans her head back against the truck seat. She doesn't look nearly as tough with mascara running down her cheeks and snot streaming out of her nose.

It suddenly occurs to me we might not be picking up a live cat. "But your cat's okay now, right?"

"Yeah. She'll be fine. It was just kind of scary, you know?"

I press another napkin into her hand. "You might want to wipe your face before you go in."

We pull into the parking lot at the vet's office, and Sassy twists the rearview mirror toward her. She peers into it and glares as she mops up.

"Thanks, Travis," she says. "I knew you'd help out."

She's back a few minutes later with Argentina, a skinny brown tabby cat with huge ears. She doesn't seem any worse for wear.

"Yay for Mom's VISA card," Sassy says. "I guess I'll be looking for extra work to pay her back. Let me know if you need a hand."

"Between you and Pippa I'm never going to be able to afford new boots," I joke.

It catches me by surprise how relieved I am to see Sassy turn a smile in my direction.

Sassy holds the cat close to her chest on the ride back to her Mom's mobile home. When she climbs out of the truck I roll down my window and call after her. "Sassy! We could use help in the paddock on Saturday."

She nods and waves. "See you then!"

I'm halfway back to the track when I realize I'm humming. The trip to the vet with Sassy has put me in a very good mood.

chapter four

On Friday morning, Ryan and I arrive at the barn before Jasper. As usual.

"They got one of Roger Downing's horses," Ryan says.

"Who got one of Roger's horses?" I ask.

"The tail thieves."

"What? They came back?"

The hairs on my arms rise.

"It was Watery Grave." Ryan takes a long pull on his coffee.

Watery Grave is a bay. His tail was black.

"Made a mess of it too," Ryan says. "Roger said they must have been in a rush because they left a bit. He said the tail looked so stupid with a few hairs left that he cut them off too."

"My little sister thinks it's people who cut up animals for fun."

"That's sick." Ryan reaches out and rubs Romeo's face. "Like some kind of devil-worshipping cult?"

"I guess. The kind of people who make sacrifices." Nasty images of skinned rabbits crowd my mind.

"I wonder if all the horses with missing tails are virgins?" Ryan says this with a totally straight face. Then he winks at me.

"Very funny."

"Hey—lighten up. Nobody's sacrificing virgins or anything like that."

"What are they doing with the tails? It's creepy," I say.

"They're probably selling them."

"Horse tails? Why would anyone sell a horse tail? To make wigs?"

Ryan shrugs. "There's got to be a logical reason. I'll check it out on the Internet tonight when I get home. Hey, Jasper. Good morning!"

"Morning," Jasper says, dragging an empty wheelbarrow behind him. "Did you hear they stole two more tails down in Barn D?"

"Two more? Other than Roger's?"

"I think they were both in Kitty's barn."

"Yeah—they were both in my barn. Green Star Rising and Peppermint Fizz."

We all turn to see Kitty McCaughran standing in the aisle. Kitty is about the size of a shrimpy ten-year-old, but she has grand-kids. She's ancient. Dad told me she started off with Thoroughbreds but moved to harness racing after a nasty wreck smashed her hip and busted a bunch of her ribs. When she walks, she swings her bad leg out to the side.

"They got you too, right?" she asks, though it's clear she already knows the answer.

Ryan nods. "Romeo."

"And that was, what—on Monday?"

"Yup."

"I'm going to write a letter to management. The suits need to do something to protect us. If morons can just walk in here and hack off horse tails..."

Kitty's voice trails off. I'm sure we're all thinking of other horrible things crazy people could do to our horses.

"What are you going to say in the letter?" Jasper asks.

"Demand more security. Maybe tell them we'll sue if anyone hurts a horse. I don't know what I'm going to do with poor Fizz. He goes nuts in the summer with the flies as it is. Without a tail? I should sue them anyway. Are you in?"

"In?" Ryan asks.

"The letter. Will you sign the letter if I write one? If all of us sign, they'll have to do something."

Ryan raises his eyebrows, and Jasper and I both nod.

"Yeah, we're in. We'll sign whatever you come up with," Ryan says.

"Good. Travis, is your dad around?"

"I think so."

"He wasn't in his barn, and he's not at The Bog."

I shrug. Before I was a Musketeer, back when I worked with my dad, I knew where he was pretty well every minute of the day. Now, I can barely keep track of myself.

"Sorry, Kitty. Good luck finding him."

Kitty limps off, and we get started. Soon we are caught up in the rhythm of the work. We clean stalls, groom horses, slide harnesses on and off and guide training carts into place. Jasper and Ryan take turns driving the horses during their training sessions. We're all paying attention to how they are feeling: if they are stiff and sore or have tons of energy or seem a little depressed. If there's a problem, we'll figure out a solution. Maybe we need to change the training routine. Maybe add some vitamins. Leg wraps. Poultices. For every problem a horse might have, we have all kinds of possible solutions. Like any team, we work together to win.

For more than a week no tails go missing. Our luck doesn't turn. We can't win a race even though it's beginning to feel like our lives depend on it. Dad said he'll wait a little longer for another payment on the money I still owe him. Chick-a-Biddy Tack and Feed has agreed to extend my credit until the end of the month. That means we have a little time to make some money before I need to pay my bill there. I guess I'm not such a big risk because the store can always keep my paycheck, but I hate owing people money.

The only good thing I've done is help Dad work on the deck. We got a ton done on Monday. That made Mom so happy she made her world-famous shepherd's pie.

It's hard to believe deck day was a week ago. The sun blazed all day. Dad and I worked in T-shirts.

Today, it's pouring. A nasty wind gusts from the north. The loose piece of tin at the far end of the barn roof flaps and thumps with each gust.

It just figures that today is my morning to drive. I'm wearing a knitted wool hat under my helmet. My old down ski jacket is puffed up, but I'm still freezing. The cold bites through my leather gloves as I hold the lines. It's too late in the season for the weather to be this terrible.

Dig in to Win clears the end of the long low side of B-Barn. A fraction of a second later a blast of wind smacks me. I'm already soaked, and we haven't even reached the track. Watching for horse traffic, we pass through the gate to the track. I turn Dig in to Win to the left so we're heading clockwise. That's the direction we need to be going for the slow part of the workout. I flick the whip lightly over his side, both lines in my left hand. I cluck at the same time. Dig in to Win springs forward, pacing easily into the rain.

Horses hitched to training carts whiz past, moving in both directions around the track. Those doing faster workouts are on the rail and traveling counter-clockwise.

I let the whip rest casually over my right shoulder, pointing backward.

Mud and water spatter the front of my jacket. I have my mesh screen visor pulled down. It snaps onto my driving helmet and helps stop the mud from hitting my face. It isn't long before my gloves are covered with gritty gray streaks kicked up from the wet gravel track. Dig in to Win settles into a steady working pace.

Pacing is a funny gait. It's different from a trot, where the horse moves diagonal pairs of legs forward at the same time. In the pace, the horse moves the front and back legs on the same side of the body at the same time. Dig in to Win wears hopples, loops that go around the upper part of each leg and sort of tie the front and back legs on each side together. The hopples remind him to pace instead of trot.

We do a few slow laps before getting down to serious business. I check over my shoulder to make sure we have lots of room and then make a big circle across the track so we're heading in the other direction. The minute we've turned around, Dig in to Win picks up speed. The horses know this is the way we go for speed, the same direction the horses race. On the curves, the jog cart pulls to the outside and I lean the other way so we don't tip or skid.

Wheels hiss through the sloppy footing. Every time Dig in to Win lifts a foot I imagine him pulling his hoof free with a little *pop*. The horse is breathing hard, the track is slow and slick. I don't want to push too fast in this mess, but he needs a good workout. We round the curve and emerge onto the straightaway. In a race, this would be the final stretch heading toward the grandstand. The finish line is along at the far end. We head straight into the wind. It's like we're running into a wall.

Dig in to Win's ears flick back and he pounds along, his hooves flying. There is a moment in each stride when all four feet are in the air. It's a moment of suspension, a wild mix of brute force and sheer elegance. His backside rocks from side to side with every stride. His tail, wet and heavy, lifts back toward me. I could reach out and grab it, if I wanted to.

I let him go all the way around again at a good clip and then take a tighter hold on the lines.

"Easy, buddy," I say, guiding him away from the rail. "Slooow down." I check over my shoulder and when there's a gap in traffic, I turn him so we're moving clockwise again.

He relaxes and slows right away, responsive and well-behaved as usual. I like driving Dig in to Win. No surprises.

The fast work over, we keep pacing steadily around the track for another ten minutes or so. Dig in to Win is fit and handles the workout with no problems. I'm the one with the problems. I'm soaked and freezing.

My dad flies past on the rail, heading in the opposite direction. I catch a glimpse of the horizontal white snip on the horse's upper lip. That's Stash, one of Dad's favorite horses. Not only is he fast, he's funny. He likes eating potato chips and paws the ground like he's trying to dig his way to China if he spots someone with a bag. He has us all trained to share.

"Let's get out of here," I say to Dig in to Win. We might have gone around another time or two in better weather. But the horse has worked well, and I feel like I'm freezing, so I pull him to a walk, and we roll through the gate.

My nose is running, and my cheeks sting when I hop off the back of the jog cart and turn Dig in to Win into the barn.

Ryan is waiting to help with the horse. Jasper has an English exam first thing this morning, so it's just the two of us.

I unhitch the jog cart and push it back to where Romeo stands in crossties, waiting. He's all ready to go, and it only takes a minute to hitch him up. There isn't much time to enjoy the relative warmth of the barn. The minute I move around behind Romeo and the cart, he starts moving. I hop onto the seat and swing my legs around as we move along between the barns. I brace myself for the blast of wind when we clear the end of the barns. Then we're on the track, and all I can hear is the *clop-clop-clop* of Romeo's steady pace, the swish of the wheels through the wet gravel and the spatter of icy rain on my helmet.

chapter five

All three of us meet back at the barn again after school. We hunch over the card table where Jasper has already marked up the conditions sheet, the list of every race that's available on the following weekend.

"I'm thinking we should move Dusty Rose up a class," Jasper says.

"Really? Why would we embarrass ourselves like that?"

"I'm with Travis on that," Ryan says, tipping his chair back. "We need a win.

She doesn't stand a chance if we move her up."

"She's a funny girl," Jasper says. "I'm thinking she'll work hard to keep up with this bunch." He points at the third race on Friday night. It's a race for fillies and mares that haven't won more than ten grand in their last five races. The claiming price is a little higher than the other races she's been in recently. The higher the price the horses are listed to sell for, the better quality they tend to be.

Ryan folds his beefy hands over his stomach. "Yeah?"

"And when we drop her back down a class the following week, she should do okay."

"It's a theory," I say. It's not unusual to bump a horse up a class to run against stiffer competition to try to get a better performance. Sometimes the faster speed will inspire a horse to come up with a personal best time, even if it doesn't stand much of a chance to finish in the money.

Sometimes the horse will have another good fast race the following week, running against horses that are a closer match. It's risky though. The opposite can sometimes happen. If a horse is too far out-classed, it can just give up and not bother trying. With Dusty Rose, it's hard to say how she'll respond.

"We don't have anything to lose at this point," Jasper says. "What we've been doing hasn't been getting us into the winner's circle."

I can't argue with that. Neither can Ryan. "Fine," he says. "Put her in."

Jasper fills in the entry form.

While he's filling out the details, Ryan studies the list of races for Friday night. "Nothing. How about we put Finnegan in the eighth on Saturday?"

The eighth is a race for horses six years old and younger that haven't won $30,000 in their lifetime. Even though Finnegan is nearly seven, he has only earned $18,978 and most of that was with his previous owner.

He was in the same race last week and finished sixth. But he was moving up and looking strong at the end. If we draw a decent post position, he might do better.

"Sounds good to me," I say.

Jasper fills out the form for Finnegan.

We have more trouble finding suitable races for Romeo and Dig in to Win. It takes nearly half an hour to debate where they will run. We wind up entering Romeo in the fourth race on Saturday and Dig in to Win in the last race on Sunday. We can only hope they get in and draw good post positions. If there are more than nine entries, we might not get selected, and we'll have to sit out. Whether we race or not, the horses need to be fed and watered and the stalls cleaned. We push back from the table and get to work.

Dusty Rose stamps her foot and paws the rubber mat in the paddock stall. It's Friday night, and we're waiting for the start of the third race.

"No patience," Sassy says. She adjusts the lightweight cooler we have draped over the filly.

"She knows it's nearly time to go," I say.

Sassy moves to Dusty's other side, ducking under the filly's head. She brushes against me. It seems to me she pauses for just a moment before continuing. "Does she know she'll make you a small fortune if she wins this one?" Sassy asks.

"She knows," I say, letting Dusty lip my open palm. "Does she care? That's another question." Dusty is the long shot in this race for good reason. We're not the only ones to realize she's out-classed in this field. That doesn't stop us from dreaming of the big upset. We all have bets riding on the race. Not big ones. We're not stupid. But if, somehow, Dusty pulls off a spot in the top three, we'd feel like idiots if we didn't have money on her. Ryan is the only one in our group old enough to legally gamble, so he's the one who takes our money and places bets for us.

"Where's Tucker?" Sassy asks, checking her watch for the tenth time in the past few minutes.

"Should be here any—Hey, Tucker. Speak of the devil. Your ears must be burning!"

Tucker Lamaze is driving for us today. He's been around forever and drives for pretty well everyone. He's in just about every race today. He trains, too, and also owns a couple of horses.

"Crazy day, Travis. Crazy day." He takes a quick look around and unzips his fly in the corner of the paddock stall.

"Tucker! What are you doing?" Sassy asks.

"What does it look like I'm doing?"

"Don't you know it's bad luck to take a leak in the stall of a horse you're racing?"

Tucker shrugs. "When a man's gotta go, a man's gotta go."

"You've got to go right now," I say, anxiously watching the other horses start to leave.

Tucker zips up, takes the lines and nods. "See you later," he says as Dusty Rose begins to move.

When Tucker is on the race bike and heading for the track, Sassy and I move to the end of the barn. A couple of propane heaters blaze close to a big TV. Dusty is horse number three, not a bad position for her to start the race. We watch the screen as the horses jog around the track, loosening their muscles, waiting for the starter's call.

Sassy bumps my side and I take half a step away, not wanting to get too far from the heater. At first, I think Sassy is distracted and not paying attention to where she's standing. But then she nudges my side with her shoulder.

I glance down and catch a sly grin sliding across her face. "I'm cold," she says, her eyes twinkling.

"How's your cat?" I blurt out. What does she mean she's cold? We're all cold.

"Argentina's fine. Thanks for asking."

Sassy reaches down and grabs my wrist. She tugs upward on my arm.

"Freezing cold," she says.

I don't have a lot of choice. My arm rises and settles around her shoulder. Sassy burrows into me, snuggling close. She says she's cold, but she feels warm to me.

My eyes never leave the screen as I pull her a bit closer. Part of my mind watches the horses on the TV make their way past the grandstand. The other part of my mind is in total shock. I hardly know Sassy. Do I know her well enough to have my arm around her? *She* seems to think so.

"Here we go," she says, craning to see.

The horn blares and the starter calls the drivers to the gate. The drivers turn their horses and set off, pacing toward the starter's car.

Harness races begin with a rolling start. As the horses approach the starter's car, the vehicle moves slowly away down the track. Two hinged steel gates stick out sideways behind the car, stretching like massive wings across the track. The horses fall into place, the numbers on their heads matching their positions. Number one is on the inside of the track. Number eight is high on the outside. The number nine horse trails just behind the number one horse, low and inside but just back a bit. The car picks up speed and we all lean forward, watching.

The horses pace quickly, their noses practically touching the gate. Just as we expect the gate to fold back out of the way, the number nine horse crowds a little too close to the number one horse. It's hard to say what happens, whether the number one horse backs off the pace a little or what, but the number nine horse falters. The wheels of the number one and number two bikes touch, causing the number two horse to fall back and get in the way of the number nine. The starter sounds the horn to recall the race.

"Interference," one of the guys watching with us in the paddock says.

"Recall," another comments.

A third chimes in with a juicy swear word.

The gate slows, preventing the horses from charging off down the track, but even so, a couple of the drivers have trouble peeling their horses' noses from the gate. These horses are pros. They know the gate means race time. It's like they want to make sure they get a good start.

"Dusty's being good," Sassy comments. It's true. She doesn't seem rattled by what happened. Tucker has turned her away and completes a big circle down to the left of the grandstand. The last horse has to be guided away by Alice, the pick-up rider who sits astride her tall Appaloosa. It's not until Alice has a good hold of the number four horse's head that the starter can try again.

While the horses get reorganized, Sassy reorganizes her hand. It slips into the back pocket of my jeans like it belongs there. I swallow hard and give her a little squeeze. She smiles and something lurches in my belly.

The horn sounds again, and the drivers guide their horses into position. This time, the number four horse, Yellow Melons, seems reluctant to move up. Yellow Melons is the favorite. She's been racing in California and doing well down there. But she doesn't like the heat. So, this time of year, the trainer moves some of his horses north just in time for the start of some of our bigger money races.

"The Melon-head thinks she's already run her race," Sassy says. Her fingers wiggle in my back pocket. "That's not a bad thing."

This time when the starter calls "Go!" and the car shoots forward, the horses get away cleanly. Right away they string out. The number two horse, Charming Eagle, moves to the front with Dusty right behind her. Yellow Melons falls way back and never rallies. The pace is slow, much slower than we were expecting from this field. Dusty stays tucked in behind the leader, looking like she belongs.

"Holy, holy crap...holy, holy crap..."

Beside me, Sassy stiffens.

When the horses pass the grandstand the first time, Dusty is still in second place. As the race continues, things start to get exciting. The field splits into two groups—five horses up toward the front and four behind. It doesn't look like any of the trailers are going to challenge. Charming Eagle seems comfortable and strong. She has a huge, easy stride and doesn't look like she's working too hard. Her driver keeps checking over his shoulder, looking for challengers. When he goes to the whip in the homestretch, he's only waving it around.

That's when the number six and number eight horses make their move. They both pull wide at the same time and charge to the finish, gunning to catch the leaders.

"Go! Go! Go!"

My heart thumps and leaps like a wild thing. What's happening? Dusty was never meant to be a contender! But she's right up there with the leaders. They race across the finish line in a flurry of whips, flying hooves and spinning sulky wheels.

Charming Eagle is the winner by a full length, but after that it's a complete mess. Three horses, including Dusty, come over the finish line practically together. *PHOTO* flashes up on the board. It will take a few minutes for the officials to figure this one out. All of us stay glued to the TV.

The results flicker across the board, and a moment later the announcer's voice echoes over the loudspeaker: "Race number three won by number two, Charming Eagle. In second, number eight, Elegance in a Box. In third, number six, High Road Dancer. In fourth, number three, Dusty Rose..."

I don't even listen to the rest of the results. Fourth? That's way better than we had hoped. We'll get some purse money, which is great. And Dusty Rose ran well. Maybe Jasper's theory was right. Maybe we'll get an even better finish next week.

"Congratulations, Travis. Can I treat you to coffee and pie? To celebrate?"

"Coffee?"

"Yeah, you know—that hot black stuff people drink?"

"Ha ha." I know perfectly well what coffee is. What I don't know is how I feel about having a cup with Sassy.

"We can't go now—," I say.

"Well, duh. I'll meet you after the eleventh race," she says. "I'm paddocking for Josh Riley in the ninth. But I'll be done by then."

She says this like she knows I will agree. What am I so worried about? It's not like it matters that she has wild hair, swears worse than anyone I know and occasionally smokes out behind The Bog. And if I'm feeling weird about keeping her warm without knowing her very well, going for coffee is a good way to fix that.

"If you're worried," she says, misunderstanding my hesitation, "don't be. I have time to grab Dusty after this race, give her a bath, cool her out and get her back to her stall. I can do all that before I come back over here to help Josh."

I nod. "Fine. I'll meet you after you're done."

"Good," she says, stepping away from me. "There's something I want to ask you about."

"What?"

She laughs. "That's for me to know and you to find out."

chapter six

I'm not prepared for the hassle I get from my partners when we all meet in the tack room after Dusty has been bathed and cooled out after her race. The minute she was done, Sassy sprinted off to Josh Riley's barn to help him in the ninth. Sassy's footsteps have barely stopped echoing in the barn when Ryan reaches over and gives me a hard slap between the shoulders.

"Putting the moves on Sassy, I hear."

I don't bother asking how he knows. Nor do I bother correcting him. Sassy is definitely the move-maker. Around here, word travels fast. Someone must have seen us cozied up while we watched the race. And someone told someone else who told Ryan. And Jasper. And my dad. And anybody else who would stand still long enough to listen to the latest gossip.

"How about that race?"

"My plan worked great, hey?" Jasper grins. He's happy we're collecting a check, even if it isn't huge. And he's happy that our mare held her own against good company.

"Coming over to my place?" Ryan asks. It's a tradition we have, celebrating a win at one of our houses. We didn't win today's race, but we're all feeling the need for a celebration.

"Ahh...I...um..."

Jasper raises an eyebrow, and then he starts laughing. "Don't tell me you've got a date! You don't waste any time, do you?"

"Travis?" Ryan's elbow nearly bowls me over.

There's no way to wriggle out of this one. "Yeah. Maybe something like that. Coffee and pie."

"Coffee and pie? Sweet apple pie?" Ryan asks.

"Or is that cherry pie?" Jasper says, barely able to stop laughing.

Ryan guffaws.

"Very funny. Maybe I won't have any pie at all. Maybe I'll stop at coffee."

Ryan and Jasper are laughing so hard tears leak out of the corners of their eyes.

"You guys are just way too funny." My cheeks burn. I'd like to run away, but that would just make things worse. "Shut up, already!"

They pull themselves together. "Make sure you top up the water buckets before you leave," Ryan says. "Jasper and I will go and have our own little party. Have fun!"

"Don't do anything I wouldn't do," Jasper adds. They head down the barn aisle, elbowing each other all the way.

What a pair of turkeys. Jealous. They're just jealous. When I can't hear them talking and laughing anymore, I get to work doing the last chores of the evening while I wait for Sassy to show up for our coffee date.

"A little coffee with your cream and sugar?" Sassy smirks when I pour more cream into my mug and give it a stir.

"It's a big mug!"

Sassy cups her hands around her steaming mug. It figures that she drinks her coffee black. "Puts hair on your chest," she says.

"Your point? Are you saying you have to shave in the morning?"

I duck sideways as a wadded-up napkin sails past my head. "Jerk!" She laughs though.

"Hey! You're the one who brought up hairy chests!" We're on our second cup of coffee, and I'm kind of shocked by how much fun I'm having. Sassy has a great smile and laughs at my dumb jokes.

I've learned a few things too. She lives with her mom and little brother in the same mobile home she's lived in her whole life. The first chance she gets she wants to quit school and go traveling. New York. Hawaii. When she was a kid, her dream destination was Saskatoon of all places.

"Saskatoon? What the heck is in Saskatoon?"

Sassy looks down in her lap and sucks in her bottom lip as if she'd like to take back Saskatoon. "I was a kid," she says. "What did I know?" Then, out of the blue she asks what I think about the missing tails.

I shake my head. "Bizarre. And cruel."

"Cruel?" she says. "It's not like it hurts the horses."

"I know that. But in the summer they won't be able to swish away flies."

"You know what I heard?" She cocks her head to one side, waiting for me to guess.

"What?"

"You can make fake tails for horses."

"With what? Stolen horse tails?"

"No, dummy. With baling twine."

"Seriously?" I can't imagine a horse with a fake tail. One made of the string that holds the hay bales together would look stupid.

"Seriously. I think the draft-horse people do it sometimes. You know, for those big-ass horses where they bob their tails on purpose."

"If the thief keeps coming back, you could make tons of money making replacement tails."

She grins. "Wouldn't that look strange? A whole race full of horses with orange and blue tails!"

"Almost as strange as a race where all the horses have bald butts!"

Sassy laughs. Sometime between cup number one and cup number two she has let her hair down. It slips over her shoulder when she tips her head back. This week the color is a rich, dark brown and all the sharp points have gone. Instead, her bangs fall loosely over her forehead, the longest strands brushing her eyelashes.

"So, who do you think is doing it?" I ask.

Sassy stops laughing. "No idea. Actually, that's not true."

"You know who's doing it?"

"No," she says quickly. "I don't know. But I have a theory."

Sassy bumps her coffee, and some slops out onto the table. She grabs a napkin and mops up.

"Well? What's your theory?"

Sassy re-wipes the table even though it's dry. "It's just a theory..."

I put my elbows on the table and lean forward. Lowering my voice, I ask again, "What are you thinking?"

Sassy glances at the door. I'm not sure whether she wants to escape or if she expects to see the tail thief standing there with a razor blade.

"Okay. You know Jasper's grandmother?"

That makes me sit up. "Jasper's granny? She's no tail thief!"

"I know that," Sassy says. "But listen, she sells those dream-catcher things at the farmers' market."

"Your point?" I can't keep the edge out of my voice. I don't like the direction this is going.

"Have you ever looked at them closely?"

"I'm not really into dream catchers."

"Why do you have one in your tack room?"

I think of the fancy dream catcher hanging from the ceiling. It's about our only decoration, outside of a couple of lonely win photos.

"Jasper brought it in as a barn-warming present when we set up shop," I say.

She acts like she doesn't hear me.

"You know the dangly parts? They're usually feathers. But that's not how she makes them."

"She doesn't?"

"Look again when you're in the tack room. Those things are made of horse hair."

"So?"

"So she sells hundreds of them. In the summer, the market is packed with tourists. She's always there, and her stall is full of the things. She must need a lot of tails to make them all..." Sassy talks faster, idly spinning her spoon on the table.

"But Jasper's grandmother never comes to the track."

"Who said anything about the old lady stealing the tails herself?"

"That doesn't even make sense! Who would–?" I stop when I realize what Sassy is suggesting. "Jasper? Forget it. No way he'd do something like that."

Sassy reaches across the table and squeezes my hand.

"I'm only saying this because I care about you. You're a sweet guy, Travis. I wouldn't want to see you get hurt."

Sassy's eyes fill with tears. I reach over and put my hand over both of ours.

"Hey," I say. Something clenches in the pit of my stomach. She looks so sad. So worried. So vulnerable. I want to move over to her side of the booth and wrap my arms around her. She'd bury her face in my shoulder and cry. I'd rub her back and stroke her hair and—

What am I thinking? I gulp down a mouthful of coffee. She couldn't seriously think Jasper would be involved with the tail thefts.

"I know Jasper," I say. "He's my friend. He wouldn't do anything stupid like stealing horse tails."

Sassy bites her bottom lip. "Maybe not for himself. But you know how Indians are..."

When Jasper uses the word *Indian*, it sounds okay. When Sassy does, it sounds wrong, almost like she's swearing.

I stiffen in my seat and try to pull my hand back. Both of her hands grip mine. The look in her eyes has changed from sad to desperate. Pleading.

"Travis, listen to me! I just want to protect you. Think about it. They live on the reserve. His family has no money. It would be easy for Jasper to—"

"No!" I yank my hand away and slide out of the booth.

"Wait!"

I throw money on the counter on the way out. She's insane! How could she say those things about Jasper? She doesn't know him the way I do!

Sassy catches up to me in the parking lot where I'm fumbling with my keys. When she throws her arms around me, she's sobbing. "I'm sorry," she says, over and over. "I know he's your friend. But maybe you're not seeing things clearly. I don't want you to get hurt..."

I stand for a long moment with my arms held stiffly at my sides. Sassy's head pushes into me, her arms wrap around my waist. "I'm sorry. I'm sorry," she moans, still sobbing.

I put my arm around Sassy's shoulders. "Hey," I say. "Stop crying." I feel her body relax against me. The top of her head reaches just below my chin. Her hair, still loose over her shoulders, smells like peaches. I close my eyes and inhale the scent.

It hardly seems possible that she could get any closer, but she manages to snuggle in, drawing me in even tighter. She pushes her hips forward and moves against me. I'm horrified to feel my jeans tighten.

"Sassy," I say, moving my hands to her shoulders to push her away.

She tips her face up and whispers, "I'm sorry, Travis. Please, please, forgive me? I shouldn't have said anything." Tears glisten in her eyes.

Before I can reply, she reaches up and slips her hands behind my neck. Her lips part, and she pulls me to her.

Oh help, help, help, I think as I reach for her and find her lips with mine.

chapter seven

We leap apart when a door slams right behind us. How could I not have heard the car pulling up? Sassy turns away and moves to the other side of my truck.

"Good cup of coffee?" Ryan asks.

Could this night get any more complicated? The passenger window rolls down and Jasper sticks his head out. Apparently, it can.

"Getting lots of cream with your sugar?" he jokes, laughing.

Ryan slaps my back as he saunters past. "Don't be late for work in the morning, my friend."

He winks and then heads for the coffee shop, Jasper close behind.

I climb into the truck and reach over to unlock the door for Sassy. She slides across the seat and cuddles next to me. I keep both hands on the wheel and my eyes on the road as we drive to her place.

When we get to Sassy's place, I still don't look at her. "Good night," I say quietly.

There's a long pause. Sassy sits still and silent beside me. "Good night, Travis," she says after what feels like forever. She reaches up and gives me a quick, warm kiss on the cheek before sliding across the seat. "See you tomorrow," she says, reaching for the door handle.

When she slams the door behind her, I drive off. Not that I get far. The minute I'm around the corner and out of sight I pull over and shut off the engine.

What just happened? My hands shake, and I sit on them to keep them still. What am I doing? What is Sassy thinking?

When I finally start the truck up again, I feel a little dizzy. At home in bed I can't fall asleep. Usually, I can't wait for morning, but tonight, things are different. I don't want morning to come. I don't want to think about being in the same place as Jasper and Sassy at the same time.

In the tack room the next morning, my cheeks burn. Jasper and Ryan have no mercy. They've been making coffee-drinking jokes and punching me in the shoulder ever since I arrived looking like I hadn't slept. There's no point in explaining that I was wide awake all night but completely by myself. The only good thing is that Sassy isn't around. I don't have to worry about her saying something dumb in front of Jasper.

"Can we try to get some work done here?" I say.

"Are you sure you don't need a nap first?" Jasper teases.

I close my eyes and slump against the wall. The truth is, I'd love to have a nap. I'm almost sorry I dragged my butt to the track. I should have stayed in bed.

"Hey, you should tell him what your mom said," Ryan says to Jasper.

"Oh yeah, you missed that yesterday. I think you were busy having coffee with someone..."

"Very funny. What did she say?"

"My mom said she'll help me apply early," he says.

I know right away what he's talking about. If you've been working around the track forever like we have, it's pretty easy to get a trainer's license when you're sixteen. But getting a license to drive in races is way harder. You have to drive in a bunch of qualifying races set up just for drivers who are learning.

There's a written test and an interview and a practical test of driving skills.

You have to be recommended by three other drivers. The list goes on and on. Then you are allowed to drive in races, but you still don't have a full license. That doesn't happen until you've survived a whole bunch of races.

Jasper has been wanting his license since he was ten. In most cases, you have to be nineteen to get your driver's license, unless a parent agrees to let you go for it earlier. My parents won't even consider it. Dad says it's too dangerous and the longer it takes for someone to get a license, the better. Not that I'm a great driver anyway. I'm just as happy training, jogging the horses to get them ready for racing. But if Jasper's mom is willing to help him get on a race bike, that's good for us.

"Go for it," I say. The Three Musketeers need all the help they can get.

"I can't believe it's going to be the end of summer before I finally get done," Ryan grumbles.

He'll be lucky to get finished by the fall. Ryan doesn't win too many races. We don't exactly have a long lineup of trainers at the door begging him to drive for them. And our own horses often race better for other, more experienced, drivers. Even *we* don't hire Ryan unless we're desperate. Jasper is the one everyone's watching. Even if he jumps through all the hoops, it's still going to be a long time before he's racing.

The rest of the weekend is a wash. Our best finish is another sixth with Finnegan on Saturday. Sassy hasn't come by, and I'm starting to think I just imagined our cozy Friday night. By Sunday evening, we're all feeling pretty grumpy.

"What are you doing?" I ask Jasper when he pulls a red duffel bag out from behind the tack trunk.

"Grabbing my duffel bag. What does it look like I'm doing?"

"Yeah, I can see that. Why? What's in the bag?"

"Sleeping bag. Toothbrush. Homework. Chocolate-chip cookies. Any more questions?" Jasper grins at me and closes the tack room door.

"Sounds like what you'd take on a camping trip."

"Bingo."

"You're going camping? What about a tent?"

Jasper rolls his eyes. "I'm sleeping right here."

"Why?"

"So I can keep an eye on the horses' tails."

Just the mention of horse tails makes me feel sick to my stomach. Sassy was the one who made the stupid comment about Jasper, but for some reason, I feel guilty. That doesn't even make sense. I wonder where she is, but then I'm glad I haven't seen her around all weekend.

"Haven't you seen the posters? About the reward?"

In fact, I have. The track bosses have offered a five-hundred-dollar reward to anyone who gives them information that leads to the arrest of the tail thief. "For once they came up with a good idea."

"Hey, five hundred bucks is five hundred bucks. We could use the money," Jasper says.

I wonder if he's suggesting I stay at the barn too. "Maybe I could stay next weekend?" I doubt my mom would be too happy about me staying here on a school night. No way I'm going to admit that out loud. I'm seventeen, not in kindergarten. But my mother is one scary woman when it comes to the subject of school.

"Sure," Jasper says. "A guy could get lonely around here at night!" He laughs. "You want to do hay or grain?" he asks, strolling down toward the feed room.

"Hay."

"I was hoping you'd say that."

Jasper is great around the horses, but he's allergic to hay. Just carrying it from the stack to the stalls makes his arms break out in red bumps. When we help unload the big hay truck, his eyes and nose stream and he sneezes for hours after. His doctor says he should wear a mask, but Jasper says he'd rather suffer than look like an idiot. I'm just glad I don't have that problem. I've never seen anyone more miserable than Jasper after he deals with a load of hay.

After all the chores are done, Jasper unrolls his sleeping bag in the tack room.

"See you tomorrow!" I call as I leave him there.

Ryan and I pull into the parking lot at our usual time the next morning. With the three of us working, it won't take long to get the chores done and all four horses exercised and back in their stalls before school.

My dad has a dentist appointment this morning, so I peel off to go to his barn first. After I feed and water his horses, his groom, Chuck, will handle the stalls and start jogging the horses.

When I'm done at Dad's, I sprint over to A-barn. Jasper and Ryan are carrying on a loud conversation while they work. Ryan is in Romeo's stall, and Jasper is out in the aisle, getting the horse ready to go.

"How'd you sleep?" I ask, grabbing the hose to start filling water buckets.

"Lousy. These damned horses never shut up."

"Didn't do much good," Ryan says.

"What do you mean?"

"The thieves got two more tails!"

"Seriously?"

"Would I lie to you?"

"Whose?"

"One from Sue Ellen's big mare. The other one was Chico."

"Chico?" I turn and look down the aisle. Chico is in Pete Hennigan's stable down at the far end of A-barn. "You didn't hear anything?"

Jasper adjusts a buckle on Romeo's harness. "Not a thing. Well, not a thing that sounded like a tail thief. I was up a dozen times, but I guess whoever it was must have done it when I dozed off."

"Dozed off?" Ryan asks. "More like bull-dozed off. I've heard how loud you snore."

"Yeah. Lucky you didn't start a stampede!" I add, pleased to be doing the ribbing for a change.

"Hey, at least I *tried* to stay awake!" Jasper protests. "Not like you two."

Ryan ignores Jasper's retort. He pushes the wheelbarrow down toward Dusty's stall. "Shall we watch our pony run?" he asks.

"Sure," I say as I snap the training cart shafts to Romeo's harness. Jasper has the lines and walks alongside Romeo when he moves off.

Jasper steers Romeo around the corner and outside. He hops onto the seat and swings his legs into the jog cart. We have to walk fast to keep up with Romeo's long, easy stride.

"Where's your girlfriend?" Ryan asks.

"She's not my girlfriend."

"Hmm. That's not what it looked like."

"Yeah, I didn't see any coffee mugs between you and that little firecracker," Jasper says, laughing over his shoulder.

There's not much I can say. "Well, it's not what you think."

"What should we be thinking, man? You looked like you were going to swallow her whole!"

My cheeks burn. For the hundredth time I wish I had never agreed to go out for coffee.

"Where is she, anyway?" Ryan asks. "You two look kind of cute together."

I shrug. How can I explain I'm relieved that she hasn't been around? A real boyfriend would be worried. A real boyfriend would have called to make sure she's okay. If I don't call, that proves I'm not a real boyfriend, right?

Jasper leaves us at the gate, and Ryan and I move over to the side to watch. Romeo jogs off down the track, his gait smooth and easy.

"How long do you think it would take for someone to cut off a tail?" Ryan asks when he sees one of the tail-less horses go by.

"How would I know? I guess it would depend if you used scissors or a razor blade or whatever."

"Did you ever find out what someone would need tails for?" I ask.

Ryan shakes his head. "My laptop died. I haven't had a chance to get online. The whole thing creeps me out. Whoever's doing it could steal anything. Maybe we should start locking our stuff up."

The idea that anyone would steal from us is just too bizarre.

"And how are they getting in past the security gate?" Ryan asks.

"This is a big place. It wouldn't be so hard to cut through the chain-link fence. Or crawl under or over somewhere."

"Unless whoever it is just strolls past security," Ryan says.

"The only people who get into the barns are people who—"

"Who work here," Ryan finishes for me.

I shove my hands deep into the pockets of my jeans. We watch Jasper and Romeo go past. Romeo's ears are relaxed, tipped out sideways. They bob gently with each stride.

Sassy's suggestion nags at me. No. Not Jasper. It couldn't be Jasper. But no matter how hard I try to erase her words they won't completely go away. I hope Jasper catches the thief, whoever it is. Then maybe Sassy will drop her crazy ideas and get to know Jasper better. Of all the thoughts that chase around and around as I watch the horses work, this last one is the strangest. If I'm thinking that Sassy should get to know Jasper, then I'm thinking I really do want to see her again. That idea is going to take some getting used to.

chapter eight

We get part of an answer to the tail question that afternoon. After morning chores, Ryan goes to the library to use one of their computers. At our weekly meeting, he tells us what he's found out.

"Did you know there are bow makers who sell these amazing hand-made bows for thousands of dollars?"

"What do you mean? Like bows and arrows?"

Ryan rolls his eyes. "No, like violins and cellos, or whatever."

"So? What does that have to do with anything?"

"You know what the string part of the bow is made of?"

"Cat guts?" I don't know where I heard that.

"Not cat guts, horse hair."

"Oh, come on! How many fancy violin bows do you think get made around here?"

"Ever heard of eBay?"

"So?"

"So someone in the violin-bow capital of the world—wherever that is—could buy horse-tail hair from right here. Why not?"

"I guess..."

"And guess what color tail hair is most valuable?" Ryan goes on. We both stare at him blankly. Then Jasper's face lights up.

"White!" he says.

"Bingo!" Ryan nods. "For making bows. That's not the only thing people make with horse-tail hair. I found these websites where people make fake tails for show horses."

"Are you serious?" I can't believe anyone would buy fake tails.

"Yeah, and they are expensive! The show people kind of blend them in with their own horses' natural tails...like hair extensions."

"No way. Really?"

"Yeah, and, there are other people who make these amazing braided ropes and stuff. I even found one place that makes these fancy rocking horses with real horse tails."

Jasper nods. He doesn't seem surprised by all the things people do with tail hair. "My grandma makes some cool stuff with horse hair, like bracelets. She does this special kind of braiding—it's kind of tricky. She tried to teach me once, but I didn't have the patience. I just get the tail hairs for her."

Both Ryan and I turn to stare at Jasper.

"Not that way, morons," he says. "Ever noticed how many tail hairs get caught in the brushes every day? I collect them for her." Jasper lifts Dusty's back hoof and picks it out. Shavings and manure fall to the ground. Ryan and I exchange a look. Then something—or someone—catches Ryan's eye.

"Well, look who's here," he says.

"Hey, boys," Sassy says. "Miss me?" Before I have a chance to say anything, she plants herself at my side and casually slips her arm around my waist. I feel like an idiot, standing stiffly beside her. Somehow, my arm floats around her shoulder.

"Hey, Sassy. Long time no see." Ryan winks in our direction.

"I've been busy. My mom needed me to babysit on the weekend. She wouldn't let me out. She's such a cow. And I had a big test in English today, so she wouldn't let me come down here before school either. I hate school. I should quit."

"Hey," I say, giving her shoulder a little squeeze, "don't talk like that."

"Be a fool. Stay in school," she says. "I missed you." She grins. "Did you miss me?"

I can feel my cheeks flushing again. I have not blushed this much since...since... well, ever.

"Jeez, Travis. You look like a tomato!" Ryan chirps up. I shoot him a dirty look.

"You want to go for a walk?" Sassy asks.

Ryan and Jasper gawk at us.

Sassy smiles up at me. "Will your bosses let you go?"

"We'll manage without him." Jasper laughs.

Once we've left the barn, Sassy takes my hand and leads me down to the far end of the barns.

"Where are we going?" I ask.

"Shh," she says. "Do you like chocolate?"

"Sure. Why?"

She pulls a bar of fancy dark chocolate from her purse and tears off the gold foil. "Here." She stops walking and snaps off a square. "Open wide."

I open my mouth and she slips in the piece of chocolate. I let it sit on my tongue for a moment before I begin to suck. "That's delicious," I say.

"I love this stuff," she says, sucking on a piece of her own. "Chocolate. Food of the gods."

We start walking again, enjoying the dark, bittersweet taste of chocolate on our tongues. There's no sound except for the crunch of gravel under our boots.

When we reach the end of the last barn, Sassy ducks around behind the building. Someone has stored some bales of hay against the back wall under the roof overhang. There's a gap between the bales and Sassy disappears into the space, pulling me in behind her. There's just enough room for the two of us to squeeze in together. She doesn't wait for me to say anything but climbs up on a hay bale, so her eyes are level with mine.

"I really did miss you, Travis," she says sweetly. Then she leans forward and kisses me. My hands reach around her waist and pull her close. She draws in a breath and then kisses me again. What choice do I have? I kiss her back. She doesn't stop me when my hands wander up her back, under her loose sweater. She sighs and pushes into me. Sassy is soft and warm and delicious. When we pull apart, we are both breathing quickly. The taste of chocolate lingers on my lips. When Sassy reaches up to touch my cheek, I catch her hand.

"Sassy...I should get back to..." My voice is husky. Dark like the chocolate we've just shared.

"What could be more important than this?" she asks, her eyes shining. Then she's kissing me again as I push my fingers into her soft hair. My nostrils fill with the smell of peaches, of fresh hay, of chocolate.

I close my eyes and every other thought disappears from my brain. All I can think of is how very good it feels to be kissing a girl as gorgeous as Sassy.

"So, I hear you and the Calloway girl are an item?"

An item? Who says that anymore? My dad, apparently. His comment at the dinner table makes both my mom and Angela stop eating.

"Ooohhh...Travis has a girlfriend?" Angela says.

"Who is she?" Mom asks.

"Ian Calloway's daughter."

"Why is that name so familiar?"

"Nasty bit of work," Dad says. "Did some time for beating up the girl's mother."

"Her name is Sassy," I say.

Dad corrects me. "It's actually Sassafras. She's named after a horse."

I had no idea.

"A horse?" Angela says. "That's crazy."

"Her dad is crazy," Dad says. "Drank too much. Gambled too much. And hit women. Ian Calloway was never a friend of mine."

"Whatever happened to him?" Mom asks. "Is he still in jail?"

"I don't think so. I thought he moved to Saskatoon. All that trouble happened when Sassafras was quite young."

"So, what's she like?" Mom asks, turning to me.

Soft. Warm. Lovely. I have no idea how to answer Mom's question.

"She's trouble, if you ask me," Dad says. He spears a piece of chicken when he says this. "Don't look at me like that, Travis. I'm just saying she's a little messed up. Who can blame her? She's had a tough life."

"People get over stuff," I say. I'm wondering about Saskatoon, whether Sassy ever sees her dad.

"Just be careful," Dad says. "Think with your head, not your—"

Milk shoots out of Angela's nose.

"Angela! Please!" Mom passes Angela a napkin. Angela's shoulders are up around her ears. She folds over in her chair, she's laughing so hard.

Not again! For the thousandth time my cheeks blaze. "I'm full," I mumble as I push my chair back from the table. A minute later I'm in my room with the door shut. Even lying on my bed with my pillow over my head I can hear the rest of my family laughing and talking in the dining room. I'm exhausted and don't know which direction to turn my thoughts. If I think about Sassy, everything is a confused mess in my head. I don't want to think too hard about horse tails or Jasper. School is something I *should* think about, but right now homework seems like the least important thing on the planet.

Like I've done for years, I think about the horses to escape from whatever else is bugging me. I imagine leading Dig in to Win from his stall, his big head at my shoulder, his huge dark eye level with mine.

The rhythmic *clip-clop* of his hooves on the concrete aisle is as familiar as my heartbeat. My breathing slows. In my imagination I lead Dig in to Win out to the patch of grass beyond the last barn. The tips of my fingers touch his shoulder. Sun-warmed, the horse's glossy coat is smooth and soft. I doze off, listening to the sound of the horse's steady chewing as he grazes on the fresh grass.

chapter nine

I wake up in the middle of the night, confused. Where am I?

It takes a minute, but then the edges of the furniture and my clock come into focus. I don't have to be at the barn for a couple of hours. The way my heart is pounding, I know that thinking about horses isn't going to be enough to get me back to sleep. My brain is so jumbled that even math looks good.

I get up and switch on the light at my desk. It turns out that trying to do my math homework is a good distraction. It's so irritating that I wake right up and stay busy until I stumble down to the kitchen to grab some breakfast and put on a pot of coffee.

Dad comes into the kitchen, sniffing the air. "Smells good," he says.

I wait for him to say something else about Sassy. Instead, he says, "Can you give me a ride to the track? Your mom is picking up the deck railings with my truck today."

Dad and I have made good progress with the deck. We even managed to finish the steps. The biggest job left is to install the railings and stain the wood. After that, Mom keeps mumbling about planter boxes and benches. She might wind up building them herself.

"Sure. Fifteen minutes?"

Dad nods and, mercifully, doesn't say anything else. Even when we're in the truck he keeps the conversation to horse supplements and whether or not the track will increase the size of the purse in the Fiddler Stakes. It's only when we're climbing out of the truck and I'm thinking I've escaped without a lecture that he puts his hand on my shoulder and says, "Just be careful, son."

Then he heads for his barn, and I head for mine. To be honest, I'm not thinking so much about being careful. I'm wondering when I might be able to find a few quiet minutes with Sassy. Now that I'm getting used to it, having a girlfriend who turns heads is great. Who wouldn't want a girl like Sassy?

I take the long way, zigzagging through the other barns, I don't see Sassy anywhere. Maybe she's waiting for me at our barn? When I arrive, Ryan is whisking a stiff brush over Dusty's back. "You're late," he says.

I try to sound casual. "Have you seen Sassy by any chance?"

"No." Ryan keeps brushing, whisking away dust and shavings and hay.

"Where's Jasper?"

"Went to get coffee. He slept here again last night."

"Any more tails missing?"

Ryan shakes his head. A dark thought pushes into my mind. If someone wanted to steal tails, staying at the barn would be a great way to throw people off the trail. Sleeping here would make it easy to help yourself to stuff. To be really tricky, you'd only steal tails sometimes. It would be too obvious otherwise.

I wish there was some way to prove Jasper is innocent. He isn't really helping his case by staying here alone. Maybe if Ryan could stay with him during the week, then I could camp out on the weekend.

"Do you think—?" I start to ask Ryan what he thinks of the idea.

Jasper strides around the corner, holding a tray of take-out coffees and a box of donuts. The words freeze on my tongue.

"Do I think what?" Ryan asks. "Hey! Donuts—thanks!" Ryan reads the scribbles on the sides of the cups. "This one must be yours, Travis—double cream, triple sugar. What were you about to say?"

"Nothing." How can I say anything about keeping an eye on Jasper without sounding like I don't trust him? I sure don't want to repeat the stuff Sassy said.

Both Ryan and Jasper take sips of their coffees. "Ah, good stuff," Jasper says. "Did I interrupt something? Were you going to talk about your new girlfriend? How did you wind up with such a hot girl anyway?"

"And where is she?" Ryan asks.

"What do you mean, where is she?"

Ryan grins. "I told her that if she showed up this morning I'd pay her to do stalls."

"What! We're broke."

"Yeah, but seeing the look on your face would have been worth it."

"You're like a puppy dog whenever she's around," Jasper says, grinning. "Yes, Sassy.

No, Sassy. You want to go for a walk? Right now? Sure, Sassy."

"It's not like that," I say.

"Woof!" Jasper replies. "Good boy, Travis."

"Shut up!" We've always joked around, but this morning, Jasper's good-natured ribbing makes me furious. Here I am trying to figure out how to prove he's innocent, and all he can do is give me a hard time!

"Ooohhh," Jasper says. "Truth a little hard to handle? Face it, man—she's leading you around by your—"

"You jerk!" I shove Jasper a little harder than I mean to. His coffee goes flying.

"What's your problem?" he says.

"For your information, I was about to ask Ryan how we could prove you aren't involved."

"Involved with what?"

"Yeah, Travis. Involved with what?" Ryan adds. They're both glaring at me now.

I get the weirdest sensation, like an icy wind is blowing through a hole in my gut. "Never mind. Forget it."

Jasper's eyes narrow. "This is about the tails, isn't it?"

I hold my hands out, palms up. "Hey, look—some people might think it's, you know, convenient that you're here by yourself all night. I was just going to say—"

I don't even get a chance to explain.

The punch comes out of nowhere and rams my cheekbone. I spin around, staggering sideways. Then Ryan is on top of me, pounding me. I swing wildly and feel my fist connect.

"You stupid jerk!" Ryan spits the words at me. Blood streams from a cut above his eye. He pulls his arm back, fist beside his ear. Ryan is breathing hard, but he's ready to come after me again.

Jasper grabs his elbow from behind. "Stop!" he says. "That's enough." Then he looks straight at me. "I thought we were friends."

"Jasper—I—" But he's not listening.

A look I can't read passes over his face. Fury. Pain. Sadness. Disbelief. Then his face closes, and I see him take a deep breath. He turns and walks away.

"What the hell is wrong with you?" Ryan says, holding a towel to his nose. After Jasper left, we moved into the tack room to patch ourselves up. I'm holding an ice pack to my cheek, and Ryan is trying to get his cut to stop bleeding. The gush has slowed down, but he's still dripping.

"I'm just saying the facts don't look good. Think about it. He needs the money. His grandma could use some of the stuff he takes. He's hanging out here every night. It doesn't look good for him."

"You are out of your mind! Jasper wouldn't do something like that."

"I'm not saying I believe it!" I really don't want to think that Jasper has anything to do with the thefts. But then again, my dad says the people who have the most to hide are the ones who protest loudest when they get confronted. Jasper was pretty mad when he stormed off.

I take off the ice and gently poke at the swelling on my cheek. "Ow." I press the ice back to my face, wincing.

I sit down heavily on the tack trunk. I still have the ice pressed to my cheek and misjudge how much room I have. Jasper's red duffel bag goes flying. He hasn't bothered to zip it up. When I reach down to grab the handle, his stuff spills out.

"You owe Jasper an apology," Ryan says.

"I didn't mean to knock it over."

"That's not what I mean."

I start to scoop Jasper's stuff back into his bag. There's a box of cookies, a binder of some kind from school, and a skin mag. I hold it up for Ryan to see and he shrugs. "Big deal. Leave the guy alone."

I toss the magazine in and reach for several large, clear plastic bags, the kind you use to freeze leftovers.

"Look at this," I say, holding out the bags.

The smallest contains several razor blades. The other contains long strands of horse hair.

"Hmm."

"Is that all you have to say?" I ask.

Ryan looks from me to the razor blades to the hair and then back at me again. Finally he says, "I'm not turning him in. The reward isn't worth that much to me."

He doesn't ask me what I'm going to do, but the unasked question hangs in the air between us. I shove the plastic bags under the cookies and the magazine and put the duffel bag into the corner with Jasper's sleeping bag.

What I want now is for Jasper to come back, so I can ask him what's going on. He's been my friend for years. He's my business partner. He's the guy who makes me laugh and brings coffee and donuts just because. I owe him that much, to hear his side of the story.

I take a sip of coffee. Even with all the cream and sugar, it leaves a bitter taste in my mouth.

chapter ten

Ryan and I don't get a chance to say anything more. Someone is singing out in the aisle.

"Hi, guys!" Pippa says from the doorway. "Got any work for me?"

"Isn't it a school day for you?" Ryan asks.

"Isn't it a school day for you?" she shoots back.

"We have hours to go before normal humans start their days," Ryan says.

"Exactly. The sale's coming up soon. May third. My dad and my uncle are both going to match however much I have saved by May second. Donuts!"

"Help yourself," I say. My appetite for donuts has disappeared.

"Mmm...chocolate glazed. My favorite." She takes a huge bite and while she's chewing she looks us over. "What happened to you guys?" she asks, still chewing.

The cut over Ryan's eye has finally stopped bleeding, but there's a big lump. A bruise is already forming around his eye. I shudder to think what my face looks like.

"We had a little argument," Ryan says, "over who has to muck stalls."

"Really?" Pippa asks, her eyes huge.

"Something like that," I say.

She looks out into the aisle. "Where's Jasper?"

"Not feeling well," Ryan says quickly. "So, yeah, we could use your help."

"Great!" Pippa says with a big grin.

"If you can do stalls and water, Travis and I will get the horses jogged."

Pippa nods and shoves the rest of the donut into her mouth. She licks her fingers and wipes them on her jeans. The three of us head out into the barn and get to work.

Ryan and I take Romeo and Dusty out together. We keep the horses side by side and give them a long, slow workout. We aren't going to ask for speed today. Usually workouts like these are relaxed. We chat about school and girls and horses, and the time flies. But today there's an uneasy silence. We each concentrate on the horse we're driving and don't say too much. We watch the other horses training, sometimes giving the other drivers a wave or a nod. I wonder if anyone else can tell how much tension there is between us.

We hear the yelling before we're even inside the barn. "I told you to get lost!" Pippa's voice carries a long way. At first I can't think who she'd be screaming at. Jasper? When I hear the other voice answer it's like someone has dumped a bucket of ice water over me. It's Sassy.

"You're stealing my job, you little jerk!" she screams.

"I am not! They hired me this morning!"

"Yesterday Ryan told me to come in!"

"Liar!"

We hop off the carts and head inside, the horses walking in front of us. "Ladies!" Ryan shouts.

The two girls turn toward us. They both hold manure rakes. It's hard to say who is angrier.

"What's *she* doing here?" Sassy demands to know.

"Where were you this morning?" Ryan asks.

"It's still morning, last time I checked," Sassy says, eyes blazing.

"Give me a hand. Hold on to him, would you?" Ryan says calmly.

113

Sassy moves to Romeo's head while Ryan unsnaps the jog cart.

"I was on my way."

"You were way late. Pippa needs the work."

"I need the work too!"

"Then you should show up on time."

Sassy turns toward me. I recognize the look. She's going to start crying.

"Ryan," I say. "If you promised her—"

"Stay out of this, Travis. When I say six I don't mean"—he checks his watch—"seven fifteen."

"My mom's car broke down again. So I had to take the bus. I missed the first one and had to wait thirty-five minutes."

"Whatever," Ryan says, pushing the cart backward down the aisle and outside.

"Travis?" Sassy has switched Romeo's driving bridle for his halter and is snapping the horse into the crossties.

Ryan is back, standing at Dusty's head while I start unhitching.

"Travis—you're an owner here, aren't you?" Sassy asks.

Why does she do this? Pit me against my friends?

"We make decisions together," Ryan says.

Sassy turns on me. "So you made this decision? To go back on your word?"

"Sassy, I never—"

Ryan glares at me. Sassy glares at me. Pippa ducks back into the stall with her manure fork.

"Do you want me to work or not?"

"Yes," I say.

"No," Ryan says at the same time.

Ryan throws up his hands.

"Well?" Sassy asks.

I look at Ryan. "Whatever." My head hurts. I don't want to deal with any of this.

"Do I have to leave?" Pippa asks from the stall.

"No, you aren't going anywhere," Ryan says. "You're the only one doing any work around here!"

In the end, Sassy and Pippa split the work and the money. Neither of them is happy about it. Neither am I, for that matter. It would have been a whole lot simpler if I'd just kept my mouth shut and we'd split the chores the way we always do.

Things get even messier after I'm done for the morning. My hand is on the door handle of my truck when I hear footsteps coming up behind me in the parking lot.

"Where are you going?" Sassy says.

"School."

"Let me rephrase that. Where are you going without me?"

She slings her arms around my waist and gives me a hug. "What happened to your face anyway?" She reaches up to touch my cheek, but I catch her hand by the wrist and stop her.

"Looks like it hurts."

"I'm fine. Do you want a ride to school?"

"Thought you'd never ask."

In the truck, Sassy slides across the seat and glues herself to my side. She keeps squirming against me until I put my arm around her. "That's better. So, where was Jasper this morning?"

I don't answer at first. "He left early."

"After he beat you up?"

"He didn't mean to—" I am about to say he didn't mean to cause the fight, but Sassy jumps in before I can finish.

"He's an Indian—violent and unpredictable."

I don't bother challenging her on that. She has said a lot of mean things about Jasper, but until just now, she hasn't mentioned anything about violence. I doubt she'd believe that he was the one who walked away, even though he thought I was accusing him of being the thief. And, apparently, I don't need to feel bad about that. That razor blade and the hair in his bag don't look good. My pulse speeds up. Stupid Jasper. What is he thinking? If he needs money for some reason, he should have asked. Not that I have any to give him, but I'm sure Ryan and I could have come up with some kind of plan. Some way to help.

"So I don't know what I'm going to do," Sassy says.

It sinks in that Sassy has been talking while I've been thinking about Jasper.

"Sorry. Do about what?"

She sighs. "You don't really care, do you?"

"I have a lot on my mind. I *do* care. What did you ask me?"

"About a car."

I really feel like an idiot now. A car? "A car for you? Did you say you wanted to buy a car?"

Sassy jabs me in the ribs. "If you'd been paying attention..."

"Sorry. Tell me."

"Yes, I want to buy a car. Not for me. For my mom. She lost her job, and her old car died, and it will cost more to fix it than to get another one, but she hasn't got any money, and my—" Sassy catches herself and stops. "I don't know why I'm telling you this. It's not your problem." She rests her head against my chest. My fingers stroke her hair.

"Maybe I can think of something," I say.

She sniffles and snuggles against me. When we pull into the parking lot at school, she reaches up and strokes my chest. "Thank you," she whispers. "I knew you'd help me."

I don't know what to say. I have no clue how to help her. Every penny I make at the feed store goes to the horses. I have a few hundred bucks in the bank, but that's for gas and truck insurance and horse bills. Besides, it isn't enough to buy a car. Why did I say I'd try to think of something?

Sassy's breath is warm and soft on my neck. She presses a gentle kiss against my throat and then another a little higher up. Her fingertips brush the bruises on my cheek so softly I barely feel her touch. Another kiss and another and then her lips find mine. By the time I finally pull free, my truck windows are completely fogged up.

"I'm going to be so late for English," I say, checking my watch.

She just laughs. "See you later," she says when I sprint away across the parking lot. I look over my shoulder to see if she's following me, but she's moving off down the sidewalk away from school. Maybe she has a spare first thing. I don't have a whole lot of time to think about where she's going, because I have to sign myself into the late book in the office, dash past my locker to grab my books and then slide into my desk at the back of the classroom. Mr. Ormand glares at me over his reading glasses and then starts talking again. Whatever he's saying is completely lost on me.

By the time the bell goes I realize I've filled half a page with doodles and thought about nothing other than Sassy Calloway, and how I'm going to help her buy a car for her mother.

chapter eleven

The rest of the day passes in a blur. The minute my last class is done, I jump in the truck and head back over to the track. Jasper isn't around, so Ryan and I do all the chores. I don't really want to talk about either of the two people on my mind, but Ryan doesn't seem to care about that.

"So, what's the story with you and Sassy?" he asks.

"The story?"

"Like are you going out, or what?"

I'm not really sure how to answer that. The time we've spent together is measured in hours and days. But I like the idea of seeing her again, even though she said some harsh things about Jasper.

"Maybe."

"Maybe? Do you have her phone number? Do you know when you're going to see her again?"

I realize I don't know the answer to either question. What I do know is I'd like to kiss her again. "What's it to you?"

Ryan puts his rake down. "Don't get me wrong," he says, "but–"

"But what?" My back stiffens. I don't want another fight.

"I don't think Sassy is the happi girl on the planet."

"Your point?"

Ryan looks pained. T' s not the kind of stuff we talk know—make people can sometim ake—"

"She's not g

123

Right then Pippa bounces around the corner. Maybe it's a good thing Sassy isn't around right now.

"Hey, Pipsqueak," Ryan says. "You want to do the last stall?"

Pippa steps forward and picks up the rake.

"Did you guys hear how fast Mashed Potato ran this morning?" she asks, stepping into Dusty's stall.

Ryan shakes his head. "Spud is back?" The tall gelding was laid up for a bit with a sore shoulder. But recently I'd seen Mashed Potato out on the track, gradually working more and more quickly. He's a trooper, one of those big blocky horses that seem indestructible. Come to think of it, his train... Beano is like that too—big and blocky and indestructible.

"One... ...y-six flat," Pippa says. "He's in the fourth... Friday night."

"Jasper... ...d Romeo in the fourth," Ryan says. ...have to watch... ...ty-six? Wow. We might... Spud."

"Give me a cut if you bet on him and win big!" With that, Pippa ducks into Dusty's stall.

"Too bad girls don't stay cute like that forever," Ryan says when we're in the tack room, out of earshot. "That kid works harder and is easier to get along with than certain other people I know. People who should be more mature."

I've had enough of his comments about Sassy. "Are we done here? I need to get over to the tack store."

"I guess so. You should call Jasper," he adds as I turn to leave.

"Why?"

"You owe him an apology."

"You know, Ryan—why don't you just butt out?"

"Because Jasper's still my friend."

The way he says it it's like there's a whole other conversation he wants to have. No way I'm sticking around for that.

"See you tomorrow," I say and head straight for my truck.

We always eat late on Thursdays. As usual, dinner is worth waiting for. At least, the food is great. Mom makes a fantastic spaghetti sauce with mushrooms and fresh peppers. There's also garlic bread hot from the oven and a big tossed salad. I'm reaching for the salad tongs when she notices my cheek.

"Travis! What happened to you?"

"Wow. Who beat you up?" Angela asks.

"Does your father know?"

"Know what?" Dad says, walking in the door. "Sorry I'm so late." He kisses Mom on the cheek and looks over at me. "What happened to you?"

I squirt a glob of dressing over my salad.

"Nothing."

"That's not nothing. What happened?"

"Are you having girl trouble?" Angela asks.

"Angela, please. Stay out of this. Travis? Answer your father. What's going on?"

"I fell."

"Against someone's fist?" Dad says, drying his hands on the kitchen towel. He sits down and scoops some spaghetti onto his plate.

"Ryan and I had a little argument."

"You and Ryan?" Dad looks at me hard. I wonder what he's heard.

"We had a difference of opinion about something."

There's a long, uncomfortable silence. Angela breaks it by giggling.

"What!"

"Does Ryan have the hots for Sassy too?"

I push back my chair so fast and so hard it rocks back on two legs. Luckily, I manage to catch it before it crashes over.

"Travis! You haven't finished your meal!"

"Not hungry," I say. I stomp out of the room.

The knock on the door comes only moments after I throw myself onto my bed. Dad pushes the door open and comes in. "What's going on with you, Travis?

Don't just lie there, staring at the ceiling. Look at me when I'm talking to you."

Dad is a patient man, but I can hear the tension in his voice. If I start to talk, I won't be able to stop. I'll have to tell him about how Sassy figures that Jasper is stealing tails, how I went through his stuff and what I found. How I didn't exactly accuse Japser, but how the evidence kind of looks bad. Then I'll have to tell him about Ryan and why he got so mad, how everyone is trying to tell me what to do, who to trust, who to like. It shouldn't be so hard to tell my dad the truth. But somehow, not a single word will come out. The whole story stays stuffed somewhere down my throat.

"You know, you'd better figure out who your real friends are, Travis," Dad says. "They are going to be around a whole lot longer than—" I put my hand up to stop him from saying anything else. He sighs and shakes his head. "Just don't let down the people who really matter." And then he's gone, the door closing behind him.

"I'm not going to, Dad," I mutter to the empty room. I will help Sassy get her mother a car. I have a plan. It doesn't matter what Dad or Ryan or Jasper or anyone thinks. Sassy needs my help, and I'm planning to give it to her. I have no intention of letting her down.

"Where's Jasper?" I ask Ryan when I drag my backside into the barn the next morning.

Ryan glares at me. "Thanks to you, moron, he's not here."

"Thanks to me?"

"He says he's not coming back to work with a racist."

The word stings, leaving an ugly mark. "What the—?"

But Ryan has already turned his back and walked away. "I'll do the hay. You can start on the stalls."

Racist? Is he kidding? I'm not a racist. I've been friends with Jasper since...since we were little kids. I never thought about him being anything except my friend until this mess with the stupid tails. I can see how hard it must have been for Sassy to say the things she did, knowing that Jasper is my friend. I feel the same way now. I want to protect Ryan, to make him see that maybe we shouldn't be so quick to let Jasper off the hook. Even if I think Jasper might have something to do with it, it's not because I'm a racist. It's because there's evidence. Just because someone's a friend doesn't mean they can't make mistakes. Why doesn't Ryan want to see that?

When Ryan gets back with the hay, he stands between me and Romeo's stall. He's too big for me to go around or shove out of the way.

"Travis," he says, holding my gaze. "You have to find a way to fix this."

"Me? I'm not the one who—"

"Do you *really* believe he did it?"

I can't say yes. I can't say no. "I—I don't know."

"You don't know? Why don't you just call the cops and turn him in?"

"How do you explain the razor blades? The tail hairs?"

"He told us he collects stray hairs for his grandma. It's not like he had a whole tail in there. And we all use razor blades—for trimming stray hairs—whatever. I don't need to tell you, of all people."

"I'm just saying we should be careful—watch him—like we should watch everyone else around here."

"You know what?" Ryan's voice is hard. "You can leave right now. I don't know what's got into you, but *you* are the problem here, not Jasper."

"You can't tell me to leave. I own a third of this operation, remember?"

"Yeah, and so does Jasper. But he's right about you. Ever since you've started hanging out with that girl, you've lost your mind."

"You jerks are just jealous because you can't find girlfriends. Sassy has more balls than you do. At least she's not afraid to ask the tough questions."

"Here's a tough question for you. How did you get to be such an ass? I don't want to work with an ass. So get the hell out of here and don't come back." He shoves me backward and pushes his face into mine. "You hear me?"

Off balance, I take a couple of steps backward. For an instant I think of fighting back, of challenging Ryan. Except Jasper isn't there to help. Which is crazy. Jasper is the last person I need to help me fight my battles.

"Fine. Do it all yourself."

Outside, shadows fill the spaces between the barns. Idiots. How did I get involved with idiots?

I'm so early for school I snooze in the truck out in the parking lot. It's not like I fall into a deep sleep, but strange fragments of dreams torment me. Ryan, coming at me with a knife. The horses getting out of their stalls and running away. Sassy turning to kiss me but then opening her mouth to reveal long pointed fangs. I jerk awake and wipe the drool from my chin. This week can't come to an end fast enough. The last place I feel like going is English class. It doesn't seem like I have a whole lot of options though. The barn is off-limits, and Mom won't appreciate me being home during the day. I grit my teeth and head into school.

chapter twelve

By the end of the day I feel like a bus ran over me. Usually, I head straight for the barn after school on Friday, but today that doesn't seem like such a good idea. The more I think about it, the more I figure Ryan will cool off. He'll realize I was right, maybe after Jasper steals something from him.

I haven't seen Sassy all day, and I don't want to call her until I have some cash. That won't happen until later tonight.

To put my plan into action, I need to be in the grandstand for tonight's races. That's where I head. There's always lots of food at the casino.

When I arrive, I pick up a copy of the race program and find a quiet table. I read over the race entries carefully and mark my bets in the margin. I've been around long enough to know which of the cashiers will take money without checking ID. Not that I've ever gambled a whole lot, but every now and then I'll bet ten bucks on a race. Tonight, though, I'll be betting more than that.

The first three races I don't even worry about: they each have four or five contenders. None of the horses really stand out. I won't waste my money. In races five, seven and eight, I have a pretty good idea who will finish well, so I calculate a series of bets. Because the horses I'm figuring will do well are also favorites, they won't pay much, but it seems like a good idea to make a little money on them while I'm busy.

The total bets on those three races is about sixty bucks. But the one I'm most interested in, the one where I'll make a killing, is the fourth.

I scan the program. There he is, Mashed Potato. I run my finger along the lines of numbers. Past performance times. Race dates and results. A hair over two minutes is his last fastest time in a real race. If Pippa's information is correct, and he posted a workout time of 1:56 flat, he's going to be right up there with the favorite, Terry Got Lucky. I check the tip sheets. *The Blue Pages* mentions the fast practice time but doesn't give him much of a chance to win. *Hoofbeater Picks of the Day*, another tip sheet that lists horses favored in today's races, likes Terry Got Lucky. Ron Charles is the handicapper who puts the *Hoofbeater* tip sheet together. He's pretty good and actually gives Romeo an outside chance of a top-three finish. The program has Terry Got Lucky listed as the favorite. The odds on Mashed Potato aren't bad: six to one.

If he wins, he'll pay off nicely; if I bet two bucks on him to win, the payoff will be about twelve bucks.

I hang around and wait as the stands fill before the evening's races. I see a few people I know, but mostly the fans are just people who show up on race day and never get anywhere near the barns. The first three races seem to take forever. And then, the fourth-race horses are on the track. I've already visited the cash machine, so I head to one of the betting windows. I read my list of small bets to the cashier. "That's it?" she asks.

"One more," I say. "Two hundred and twenty dollars on Mashed Potato to win in the fourth."

"That will be two hundred and twenty dollars." I feel queasy when I hand over the stack of twenty-dollar bills. I've never bet this much. But if it works out the way it should, I'll have more than enough money to make back my investment and give Sassy enough to either get a cheap old car for her mother or pay the repair bill on the one she already owns.

I gather up the tickets and move to a spot at the end of the grandstand nearest the finish line.

The race gets off to a good start. Eight horses pace strongly behind the gate, their noses tight up against the wings. "They're off!" the announcer calls, and the starting gates fold away as the car races off ahead of the horses. The starting car pulls well to the outside of the track and follows the horses as they drop down to the rail and settle in for the first lap. Mashed Potato is right out in front, setting a blazing fast pace. Romeo is tucked into second place with two horses right behind him. The speed is too much for him though. By the time the field sweeps past the grandstand the first time, he is falling back and the number seven horse is making a move on the outside. The seven horse passes three others before dropping to the rail for the turn. My stomach clenches and my heart thuds so hard it feels like it is swelling with every beat. *Thump. Thump. Thump.*

On the far side of the track, two drivers take their horses wide, challenging from the outside. Romeo has dropped way back, but I'm not watching our horse. I'm nodding and swaying forward, rocking as if I were in the sulky myself, driving the horse toward the finish line. "Yes," I whisper, my mouth dry. "Go..."

Mashed Potato's driver snaps the whip as the horses round the final turn and drive down the stretch. They are flying, manes and tails streaming. Whips crack and several of the drivers lie way back in their sulkies. Then, the worst happens. Mashed Potato breaks his stride, bursting into a gallop. Short of getting into an accident, breaking stride is one of the worst things that can happen in a race. Trotters must trot and pacers must pace—but neither are ever allowed to gallop. That's the whole point of harness racing—to see how fast horses can trot or pace.

Mashed Potato's driver checks over his shoulder and finds a hole to move him to the outside, out of the way. The driver fights to pull the horse back to the pace. Inside, horse after horse flies past. Mashed Potato drops back into a pace again and surges forward, but the effort is much too late. There is no way to make up the lost time and ground. He finishes dead last. Even Romeo manages to beat him.

I try to swallow, but my mouth is so dry I can't. The betting tickets are crumpled in my fist. I force myself to look at them. None of the horses I picked came in the top three in any combination. I have just thrown away $220. Oh my god. That money was supposed to be going toward a new horse. Or emergency vet bills or feed bills or truck repairs. I don't even want to think about how hard it was to save that money or how little there is left in my account. For a moment, I consider taking out whatever I have left in the bank to try again. But I know there's no point in staying for the rest of the night. The fourth race was the sure thing. And look what happened to that.

On Saturday morning I have a strange problem. I am up at my usual time, but I have nowhere to go. Ryan made it pretty clear he doesn't want me around. The truck drives itself to Sassy's place. The light is on, so I take a chance and tap quietly on the front door.

At first there's no answer, so I knock again, a little louder. The door opens a crack.

"Who's that?" Sassy's mother says, peering through the narrow gap. "What do you want?"

"I–I–" Has Sassy even mentioned me to her mom? "I'm Travis. I know Sassy from the track. I thought I'd see if she wants a ride."

The crack widens. Mrs. Calloway wears a fluffy red bathrobe two sizes too big for her. Her hair is streaked blond and pulled up into a messy bun high on her head. Smoke curls from a cigarette she holds in the same hand as a Mickey Mouse coffee mug.

"She's in the shower. You can go wait in her room."

The door opens, and I hesitate. "Hurry up. You're letting the cold in."

"Who's there?" a man's voice calls from the living room.

"Go back to sleep, Ian," Mrs. Calloway calls back. She leads me down a narrow hallway and pushes open the door into Sassy's room. "Wait in there," she says.

The door closes behind me, and I find myself trapped in Sassy Calloway's bedroom.

The room is small but doesn't seem crowded. Even though it's early, Sassy has made her bed. A stuffed giraffe sits on a faded patchwork quilt. I sit on the edge of the bed and wait.

The sound of running water stops, and I try not to think too hard about Sassy naked and dripping wet in the next room.

Watching the screensaver on her computer helps distract me. Photographs of horses, friends pulling faces and some blurry photos of her cat float across the screen. Not all the photos are turned the right way. I lean sideways to see if I recognize anyone in a photo taken at the track. The door opens and Sassy yelps like she touched something hot.

She pulls the door closed and whispers, "What are you doing here? How did you get in?"

"Your mom let me in."

"My mom? You talked to my mother?"

"Well, I hardly talked to her. She just said to wait here for you. Your hair looks cute like that."

Sassy reaches up to touch the mountain of bright red and yellow towel piled on her head.

"What are you doing here?" she says again. She glances at her alarm clock. "Shouldn't you be at the track?"

"I thought you might want a ride—"

There's a crash out in the living room. Sassy's eyes widen and her hand covers her mouth. There's another thump and Sassy's mother yells, "Shut up!"

"No daughter of mine is going to–" The man's voice is loud, angry.

There's another crash as something falls over.

"Is that your dad?"

Sassy chews her bottom lip and glares at the closed door. "He's such a jerk."

Out in the living room, the argument is getting even louder. "You've got no control over that girl!"

"She's none of your business! You walked out on us! You have no right to interfere."

"Walked out! Whose fault was that?"

"Should I go and–," I ask, not sure what I'm offering to do.

"No," Sassy says. "We should leave." She pulls the towel off her head and sweeps her wet hair back into a ponytail. She reaches into her closet to grab a sweater. Another loud crash comes from the living room.

"Damn," she says. "My purse is in the kitchen. Wait here."

Out in the living room, her mother and father keep yelling. They aren't even listening to each other anymore.

"I never asked you to come back! We were just fine without you!"

"Like hell! Look at this dump!"

"Don't touch me, you jerk! Get out!"

Then I hear Sassy. "Can you two just stop!"

"Don't you talk to me like that!" Sassy's dad roars.

I stand, ready to rush out and help Sassy.

"What are you going to do? Hit me?" Sassy yells. She follows up with a string of curses.

All three of them start screaming at each other. I have no idea what to do. I take a step forward, my heart pounding. If I go out there, I might make things worse. It doesn't sound like anyone's getting hurt, so I decide to stay put.

I look around the room for a potential weapon in case things get ugly. That's when I see the cardboard box in the bottom of the closet. At first I think an animal, maybe a cat, is curled up asleep inside. When I lean forward to take a closer look, I can see what's in the box: horse tails neatly bundled and fastened with yarn.

I jump back when the bedroom door swings open. "Let's go," Sassy says. "Now." She's already back out in the hall, but I'm still rooted to the spot, stunned.

"Travis!" she says. "Let's get out of here!"

The edge in her voice gets my feet moving.

Outside, Sassy grabs my arm and hurries me down the steps. The sky in the east is just starting to lighten. Her parents are still yelling.

"Shouldn't we call someone?" I ask, still reeling over what Sassy has in her closet.

"Get in the truck," Sassy answers.

I open the door and she jumps in. I put the key in the ignition but don't turn the engine over. "We can't just leave your mom in there." I reach for my cell phone.

"Don't," she says. "It's okay."

"It's not okay," I say.

The mobile home's front door opens, and Sassy's dad stands silhouetted against the yellow kitchen light.

"Get the hell out of here! Scum!" Sassy's mother points down the road. "Get out of my sight!"

Sassy's dad's fists are balled at his sides. He backs down the steps and stalks off down the sidewalk. He doesn't exactly walk a straight line, but he moves pretty fast. We watch him until he gets to the end of the block and turns the corner.

When I look down at Sassy, her cheeks are shiny and wet. "I'm so sorry, Travis," she says and sinks against me.

My stomach clenches. How did she get the tails? Why is her dad back at home?

The answers will have to wait. She's so upset she's shaking.

"I'm sorry, Travis," she manages to get out through sobs.

I put my arm around her shoulders. "Hey, come on." I want to tell her there's nothing to be sorry about. But I'm thinking that's not true.

"I'm sorry you had to see that—see—him."

The last word catches, and she starts to cry harder. Her fists jam against my chest when I try to hold her. The noises she makes are awful—like an animal or someone who has never learned to speak. They come from way down deep. All I can do is hold her and rock her gently until she begins to relax.

The sun is up when she finally stops. It seems cruel to start asking her questions when she's still sniffling and breathing in little hiccups.

"Can I buy you breakfast?" I ask.

"I'm such a mess," she says, looking in the rearview mirror.

"Nobody will care," I say. "I don't care. I need a coffee—and bacon and eggs and fried tomatoes."

"We're not going to The Bog, I guess."

I shake my head. "I'll take you to Charlotte's."

She musters up a little smile and nods. "Their home fries with onions are really good."

chapter thirteen

Charlotte's Café is already busy. Truckers, construction workers, a few track people and some college students lean over steaming plates of food and oversized coffee mugs. We're lucky to get a little table in the back.

"I didn't think your dad lived here," I say, hoping to get a bit more information before she realizes I know that she has the tails.

She looks at me over the top of her frothy hot chocolate. "He didn't. Oh, Travis—I've messed everything up."

"It's not your fault he's—he's—"

"A jerk? No, that part isn't my fault. But I'm the one who found him and asked him to come home."

"You asked him to come back?"

The waitress brings our plates. "Can I get you anything else?"

"Hot sauce, please," Sassy says.

After the waitress drops off the bottle, Sassy continues. "You wouldn't understand. Your family is so nice. It was so hard with just me and Mom and Brandon. Trying to work and go to school. The last guy Mom was seeing was such a jerk."

"Is he your brother's dad?" It's getting hard to keep everyone straight.

Sassy shakes her head. "That was another guy. We haven't seen him since Mom was about four months pregnant."

I nod. What am I supposed to say to that?

"Anyway," Sassy continues, "I just wanted—I don't know—a normal family. So I found my dad on the Internet and asked him to come back."

"And he did? Just like that?"

Sassy suddenly can't meet my eyes.

"Sassy?"

She turns back to me. "You're going to hate me."

Even though Sassy's life is way more messed up than I thought, I don't think I can actually hate her. "I won't hate you," I say.

"I kind of pretended to be my mom."

I lean back in my chair. "Wow."

"And he believed me. So then I had to pretend to my mom that Dad had contacted me and that he was really sorry and wanted to come back..."

"Your mom believed you?"

"Well—it's just, I know my mom. She doesn't like to live alone. And, yeah—she told me my dad was an ass, but, well—she says that about all the guys she's been with, even when they're not that bad. She still has this photo of the three of us. It's in the living room. And once she told me that my dad was the love of her life. Of course, she'd been drinking when she said it, but I always wondered, you know, whether things would be different, if he could have changed."

"Eat up," I say, pointing at her food. She's barely touched her breakfast.

"I'm sorry. I'm really not that hungry."

She heaves a huge shuddering sigh and pushes her plate back.

"But he hasn't changed at all. And he won't leave. So I figured if I could get some money together, I could get a place of my own. Even renting a room somewhere would be better than being at home. I'm tired of my mom's craziness. And my dad— well, you saw him...I need to get away."

A knot wraps tight in my stomach. "So *that's* why you needed the money?"

She looks trapped. "I didn't think you'd want to help if you knew..." She shrugs.

It's time to tell her what I know. "And that's why you stole the tails?"

The way her chin snaps up and her eyes fly open I know I'm right.

I half expect a blast of furious words or more tears, or something worse, but she just slumps back and closes her eyes. "Oh, Travis. What am I going to do?"

I shake my head. What a mess.

As we sit there in silence, I have the same helpless feeling I get when a horse goes down and you know there's not much you can do to save it. But this time it's a person who's down. Not only that, I have the awful feeling that this relationship is going to be tough to save. What surprises me most is the sting of tears now that I know the truth. I blink and gently pull my hand back.

"How did you do it?"

At first I think she's not going to answer. She stares down at the table, the muscles in her jaw working.

The time it takes for her to answer is long enough for me to pull my thoughts together. Sassy has been lying to me from the beginning. A bubble of anger pushes up through the layers of hurt and disbelief. Sassy tried to turn me against my friends.

When she finally starts to mumble an explanation, I'm so mad I can barely force myself to sit still and listen. I make myself stay and hear her out. I want all the details so I can tell Jasper.

"It wasn't hard," Sassy says so quietly I need to lean forward to hear. "Mom doesn't care if I'm out late. Like she could stop me. I went to the track early enough that people were still around, as if I had to go to work. Then I'd hide out until late and wait until everyone had gone. There are lots of places to hide."

She flicks a quick look in my direction. I think of the space between the hay bales where we shared chocolate and kisses. Was that one of her hiding places?

Her gaze drops back to the table. "Rainy nights are best," she continues. "Nobody hangs around, and whoever is on the gate stays inside the hut. Getting the tail is quick, once I'm in the stall."

"How do you see what you're doing?" I can't imagine she'd turn on the overhead lights.

"I have a headlamp. I only turn it on for the few minutes when I'm in the stall— working. When I'm done, I stick the tail in my backpack."

She looks up at me again. "I'm sorry. I would have told you...I wanted to tell you."

I don't bother saying anything. We both know that's just another lie.

"What are you going to do?" she asks.

It's my turn to shrug. I have no idea.

"Right now, I need to get to the track," I say. "Do you want me to take you home?"

She nods and her eyes fill with tears. This time, though, I feel no desire to put my arm around her. "Come on," I say. "Let's get going."

When I drop Sassy off, I get her to run in and get the box of tails. She doesn't argue. It's like all the fight has gone out of her.

I leave her standing on the top step out-side her door and head for the track alone. In the parking lot, I throw an old towel over the tails and stuff the box under my arm.

When I get to our barn I say, "Don't say anything until you hear this." I march past Ryan and Jasper, who follow me into the tack room.

"You're not supposed to be–," Ryan starts to say.

I pull the towel away. Ryan and Jasper look at the tails and then at me.

"Where did these come from?" Jasper asks.

"My ex-girlfriend."

Ryan lets out a long low whistle. "Sassy?"

I nod. For a long moment, nobody says anything. Jasper is the first to break the silence.

"I guess that explains a few things."

"Yeah—like why Sassy was trying to put the blame on you," Ryan says.

Jasper nods slowly. Any thought that I'm going to get off easy disappears when he speaks again.

"We all know that Sassy is a little messed up. What I don't get is why you went along with it. How you could believe the things she said about me—being a thieving Indian and all that?"

"How do you know what she said?"

Jasper looks at me like I'm stupid not to know. "Let's just say that girl has a big mouth. You don't think you're the only one she's been talking to, do you?"

I let that sink in for a moment. "Okay—she might have said some stuff. That doesn't mean I believed it."

"Keeping your mouth shut is nearly as bad as saying ignorant stuff yourself."

To my surprise, Ryan starts to defend me. "Travis has been...distracted," he offers. "He hasn't shown the best judgment."

I can't argue with that.

"And there was some evidence—like the tail hairs and razor blades he found in your bag."

"You went through my stuff!"

Jasper looks like he might come at me. I take a step back.

"Your bag fell over and stuff fell out. Stuff like tail hairs and razor blades," I say, trying to explain.

"I told you already. I collect stray hairs for my grandma. There's no way I'd chop off whole tails. And the razor blades go with this."

He reaches up and grabs the bottle of coconut oil from the shelf above the card table. "One word," he says. "Chestnuts."

"Oh." I felt bad enough before, but now I feel really dumb. Jasper has a thing about chestnuts, the horny growths on the inside of a horse's legs. He has a technique for getting rid of them. He uses coconut oil to soften the chestnuts and then he carefully slices them off with a razor blade.

They don't bother me enough to fuss with them, but Jasper can't stand them.

"We're almost out," he adds, holding the nearly empty bottle and looking at me meaningfully.

"Fine. I'll pick some up. And—"

"And?"

"And I'm sorry." The words are out there, but like my dad says, apologizing only goes halfway to fixing things. The other half is the tough part, doing something to make things right.

"I'm not going to see her anymore," I say.

Jasper almost looks like he's going to protest, but I put up my hand. "She did something stupid when she stole the tails—but I kind of understand why."

I explain about Sassy's parents and how desperate she is to raise the money to move out.

Ryan and Jasper nod and ask a couple of questions but mostly they listen.

"Stealing isn't the worst thing though," I say, looking straight at Jasper. "She should never have lied and tried to get me to blame you. And I should have walked away the first time she said anything about—"

I look down at the hole in my boot, shame bringing a flush to my face. How could I have been such a moron?

Jasper sighs.

"If it makes you feel any better, she also managed to get me to clean out my bank account." I tell them about the bet on Mashed Potato.

"Jeez, man—she really had you wrapped around her little finger," Ryan says.

"She did," I agree. "So, what should we do?" I nod over at the box of tails.

"I guess we should tell the guys in the office," Jasper says.

"She shouldn't really be working around the track," Ryan says. "Who knows what she'll try next."

I nod glumly. Even after everything that's happened I know a small part of me will miss Sassy.

"Don't look so miserable," Ryan says, whacking my shoulder. "We could use the reward money."

Jasper laughs. "That's for sure."

I nod, but I don't want any of the reward money for myself—not for turning Sassy in.

"Hey! I heard there's a cute girl who just started working for Kitty. We could get you two introduced," Ryan says with a wink.

"Don't give him any ideas," Jasper fires back. "The man has no self-control."

Just like that, we start joking around again. Ryan pulls the tack room door open, and we spill out into the barn aisle, ready to get back to work. I don't know what will happen to Sassy. She'll be banned from the track for sure, but I hope she doesn't get arrested. What I do know is that I'm not the right person to help her. At least, not right now.

On Saturday, the three of us scream our lungs out as we watch Dusty Rose fly over the finish line, a full length ahead of the horse in second place. Jasper and I exchange high fives and Ryan actually hugs me. We scoot over to the winner's circle, and the owners of Three Musketeers Racing Stable line up to get our photo taken with Dusty. The photographer raises her camera, and Jasper shouts, "All for one and one for all!"

The flash goes off, catching us all laughing. When we get our copy of the photograph, I'll have it framed and hang it right beside Jasper's dream catcher. I can't think of a better way to celebrate the win.

Nikki Tate is the popular author of many books for children, including *Jo's Triumph* and *Jo's Journey*. Nikki (and her collection of goats, ponies, dogs, cats, and assorted feathered friends) makes her home on Vancouver Island. Her first book in the Orca Sports series was *Venom*.